# DARKEST MOON

## SHADOW GUILD: WOLF QUEEN

### LINSEY HALL

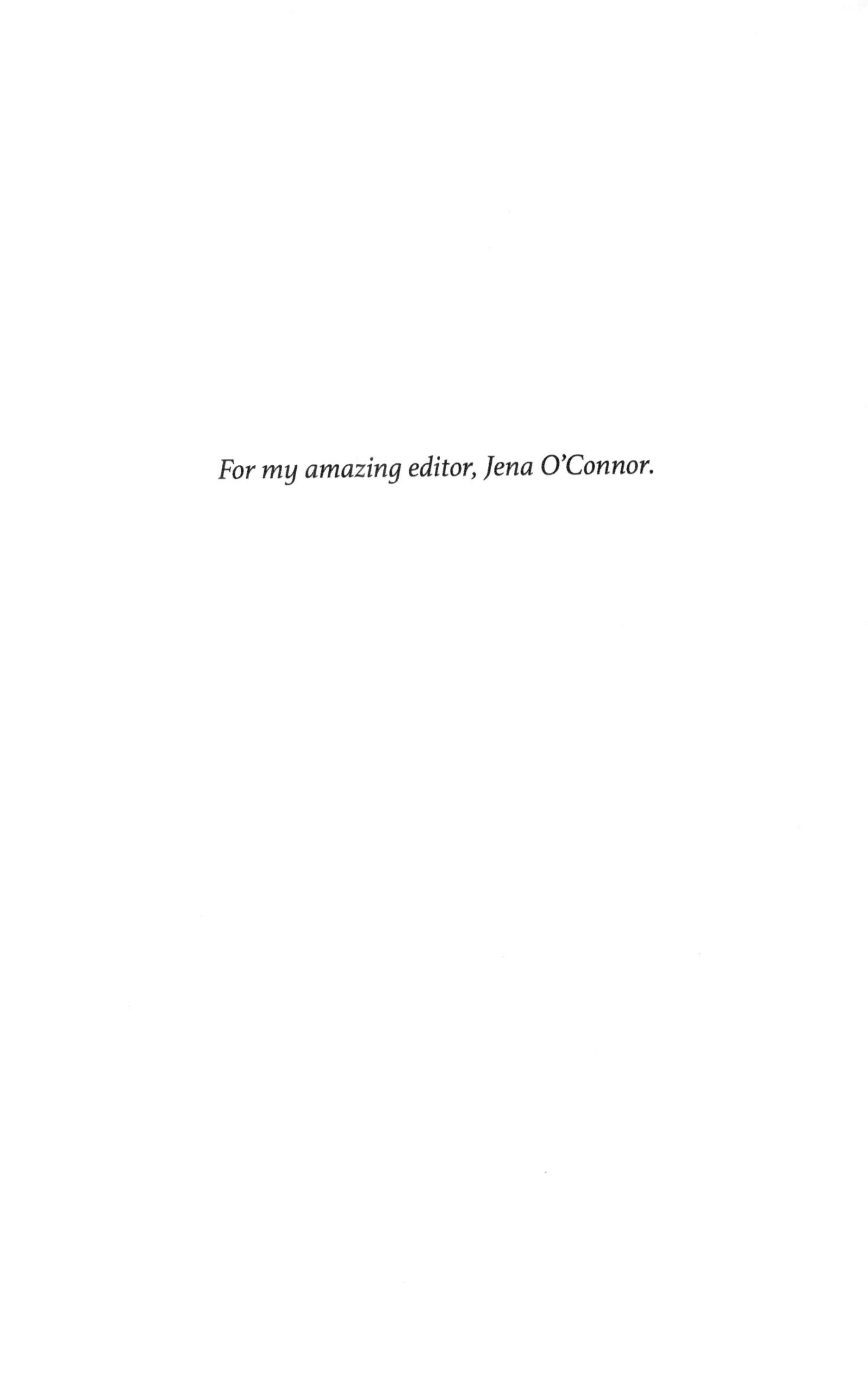

*For my amazing editor, Jena O'Connor.*

# GUILD CRESTS

# 1

*Eve*

Today was *the day*.

The day I dreaded all year.

I looked up at the row of shops and bars that lined the street across from me. Music blared from the club in the middle of the row, and a hulking bouncer guarded the door.

I reached into my pocket and grabbed a mini chocolate bar. In seconds, I had it unwrapped and shoved in my mouth. Chocolate couldn't fix my situation, but it sure as hell could help. When I was nervous, I scarfed chocolate like a frantic hamster, cheeks full and eyes intense. It was not one of my finer qualities.

But I couldn't be blamed. Not when it was time to pay the blackmailer who'd been on my arse for years.

This time, he insisted on meeting at Pandemonium, the underground fight club run by the shifters of Guild City.

Therein lay the problem: the fight club was on the *shifters'* turf.

I hadn't been back in their part of the city since I'd left in the dead of night, ten years ago today. Staying away was the only way to stay hidden.

My big secret? I was supposed to be the Alpha's fated mate. I just didn't want anyone to know.

"Get it together," I muttered.

I shook off my nerves and walked toward the club, reminding myself that I was totally unrecognizable as the girl I'd once been. Growing up had been kind to me, turning me from a legit ugly duckling into a—well, not a swan, exactly, but I looked nothing like I had. Plus, I wore a charm that hid the fact that I was a failed shifter. I looked like a fae now, pointed ears and everything. No one would recognize me.

Still, every inch of me vibrated as I stopped in front of the bouncer. The disdainful look he swept down my form made me reach for another candy bar. I stopped before taking it out of my pocket, knowing it would be insane to eat it while making eye contact with him.

"Hey, weirdo," he said. "Saw you standing across the street staring at the place, shoving chocolate into your gob. You trying to satisfy an unfulfilled need of some kind?"

Oh, wonderful. I was going to have to actually speak to this man. He was enormous, with pale skin and a crooked nose that had probably been broken a few times. The words *Lost Warior Soul* were tattooed on his neck. Did he know it was misspelled?

"Listen, if you've got unfulfilled needs, you might as well admit it." He stuck out his tongue and waggled it. "You're not really my type. I like classy birds. But I take on the odd pity case."

"Well, that sounds like quite the treat. Must've worn my lucky socks today. But sadly, I've got to get inside. Are you going to let me in?"

His lip curled. "Sorry, this is a nice place, I'm afraid. Where'd you get those clothes? Clearance sale at Primark?"

Humiliation burned through me. Memories of being a kid and getting bullied for being poor and ugly flashed in my mind. To make matters worse, the Alpha—the one who was supposed to be my mate—had been the cruelest of my tormenters.

"I can change my clothes," I said. "You're stuck looking like a right idiot with a misspelled word permanently on your neck. Was it cheaper to leave out the second R on *Warrior*?" I tutted. "The state of you. Honestly. Now, are you going to let me in or not? I know it's not actually that classy."

"You still look like a charity shop case." He glared at me as he opened the door for me.

I rolled my eyes and stepped forward. The top floor was just a bar, same as any other. Beer, bartender, patrons on stools. It was a bit darker and had a more dangerous vibe than my usual place, but nothing I couldn't handle. There were only two people at the bar, both slouched over tumblers of amber liquid.

The bartender looked up, meeting my gaze with uninterested eyes. It was fight night, so people weren't there for the drinks. I remembered enough of that from my brief youth, along with where I needed to go if I wanted to find the action.

I nodded once and turned toward the stairs at my left. The noise echoed up from the room below. Before descending into the crush of people, I made sure the envelope of cash was safe and that my pocket was buttoned. Inside that envelope was every penny I'd scrounged up over the last year.

I took the stairs two at a time, determined to get this over with.

Step one of hiding in plain sight: don't act afraid.

When it came to hiding, my necklace helped, but attitude was half the battle.

And I had it.

Gritting my teeth and squaring my shoulders, I walked down the last few stairs and into the crush of people.

And immediately had a panic attack.

There were dozens of them, all crowded around the raised fight ring in the middle of the room. Sounds and scents and heat crushed into me.

I'd spent ten years hiding from my pack, and now I was surrounded by them. My pack. Once, my family. My head spun, senses in overdrive.

*Get it together.*

I grabbed one of the chocolates from my pocket and popped it in my mouth, chewing quickly. Calmed, I pushed my way through the crowd toward the bar. If I ordered a drink, I'd have a logical place to stand while scouting out the crowd.

The bar was crowded, but I managed to squeeze in between two guys to find a spot. One of them turned to me, interest in his pale eyes. All I had to do was turn on my Resting Bitch Face to make him flinch and turn away. RBF was key to encounters like this.

I leaned over the bar and caught the bartender's attention. She was a tall, slender woman with a mop of purple hair and sharp eyes.

Fear immediately stabbed me in the stomach.

*Clara.*

A bully from school.

My heartrate rocketed as I smiled at her, and I drew in a slow breath through my teeth, trying to calm myself while not looking like a maniac.

She stopped in front of me, a polite smile on her face. "What'll it be, love?"

"Pint of lager. Cheapest kind."

She nodded and turned to the taps. Cold sweat raced down my back as I held myself steady.

She hadn't recognized me. And she wouldn't.

I was right.

When she handed off the beer, I gave her the money and turned away, studying the crowd.

Was Lachlan one of the people in the crush?

No. He was the Alpha, for fates' sake—too busy and important to be hanging out at an underground fight club.

The fight in the ring had ended, and people were jeering or cheering, depending on their alliance. There was plenty of betting going on, and the emotion in the room was high.

Immediately, a sense of *home* washed over me.

I ached for it.

For all their faults, shifters were fundamentally good. Loyal, passionate, warm. Fierce when they needed to be, protective of those they loved.

I'd left it all behind, but that didn't mean I didn't mourn for it.

Shit, I needed to get my act together.

Fortunately, my gaze landed on the rat bastard himself: Danny Walker, who had figured out my secret. I'd tried to convince him to meet anywhere but here, but he'd been utterly terrified of leaving their land, which was new for him.

He stood in the shadows about halfway to the ring, his face pale and gaunt. He looked like hell, actually, like he hadn't slept in a month. Danny had never been attractive, but this was rough.

Whatever. Didn't matter.

I would pay off the bastard and return to life as normal, scraping by but happy, mostly. Free, definitely.

I pushed my way through the crowd, ready to get this the hell over with.

As I neared him, a new figure climbed into the ring. He was tall and broad. The curves and planes of his muscles glinted under the light, so perfect that he could have been carved by the gods themselves. When he turned to me, I caught sight of his face. Beautiful. Brutal. Harsh angles and full lips, piercing dark eyes. A poet's face and the body of a warrior.

The sight of him knocked me in the gut.

Lachlan MacGregor.

My head went light.

Oh, God, I'd been a sucker to agree to meet here.

The whole point of paying off the blackmailer was to avoid the eye of Lachlan MacGregor, the Alpha of the entire pack. My fated mate.

The one I'd run from as a teenager.

I'd barely known him then, but the memory of his words still cut.

When I'd been fifteen, our most respected seer had prophesied that I would be his mate, and that the bond would somehow kill me because I was an abomination. She wasn't wrong about the abomination thing. I had no beast inside me, the way the others did. The Alpha's mate was meant to be a pure wolf, and I couldn't even shift.

I'd known then that I needed to run. If I stayed, my best-case scenario was being forced into matehood with the guy who had been so cruel to me. The worst case, as ordained by our most powerful seer? My death.

So yeah, I'd run.

Lachlan's gaze landed on me, and heat flushed through my body, followed by fear. A connection tightened the air between us, something I hadn't felt in years.

Before I could tell if recognition flashed on his face, four other figures climbed into the ring, each with their knuckles taped. He turned to face his opponents.

Four against one.

I wasn't surprised. He'd been a kid when I'd seen him last—eighteen to my fifteen—but even then, he'd been strong.

Didn't matter. Only one thing was important here: pay up, get gone.

I turned and pushed my way to Danny. The sound of the fight broke out, but I didn't look.

Danny spotted me a half second later, his eyes flashing. He looked twitchy as hell, more so than usual, and clutched a tumbler of whisky in his hands.

"About time." He thrust the glass toward me. "Here, hold this. I need a smoke."

"You can't smoke here." I took the glass because he looked like he might drop it and watched as he dug around in his pockets.

"Don't care."

"Do it after I'm gone. I don't want attention." I shoved the glass back at him, and he took it, scowling.

"Fine." He swigged back a deep sip.

I unbuttoned the pocket of my jacket and reached in for the envelope of cash. Danny's eyes widened, and I frowned. Suddenly, he grimaced, his face twisting, then collapsed and landed on me like a sack of rocks. I went down hard, trapped underneath him.

"Danny!" I hissed, pushing at his shoulders as I tried to get him off me. "What's wrong?"

"The bastard got—" He drew a gurgling breath, then went still.

So still.

Cold rushed over me, dousing me in ice.

Danny was dead, and I was trapped.

*Eve*

For one brief, blissful second, my mind went totally blank with shock.

Then the reality of my situation hit me.

I was flat on my back in Pandemonium with a dead shifter on top of me. Terror gave me the strength to push him off me, but it was too late.

A ring of shifters stared down at us, a dozen faces creased in surprise. Their surprise turned to horror as they caught sight of Danny's face. Pale green foam spilled from his lips.

"Poison!" A woman pointed at Danny, her eyes wide. "He's been poisoned!"

*Oh, no.*

Dread uncurled in my stomach.

"Doesn't she run that potion shop in town?" another voice whispered. "I swear I recognize her. Her hair is always a crazy color."

I scrambled to my feet, heart thundering in my ears. I had to get out of here.

The shifters closed ranks, tightening the circle that surrounded me. I was an outsider, and they were a pack.

"You poisoned him." A bulky man pointed his finger at me. "You *killed* him, you evil witch."

"Fae," the man next to him said. "Pretty sure she's fae. I've seen her with wings. Sparkly things. And look at those ears."

I wasn't fae. That was just my cover, a disguise that I'd created with the help of potions. It was incredibly difficult magic—impossible, almost. But I couldn't tell them that.

"I didn't hurt him!" I gestured down at Danny. "I didn't do anything to him. We were just talking, and then he collapsed."

"He gave you his glass," a pretty woman said. She was pale and slight, with keen eyes and an intelligent face. "I saw him. You slipped something in it."

Panicked, I looked for an escape through the crowd. There was none. I'd come here with backup plans and some potion bombs that could help me out in a pinch— a freezing potion, a forgetfulness potion. But I'd never considered that the *entire pack* would turn against me.

I backed up, trying to get away from the ones staring at me. Hands pushed me from behind, and I stumbled, going to my knees.

My heart leapt into my throat, fear icing down my spine. Would they tear me apart right here? No. shifter law could be brutal, but that was over the top.

"What's going on?" a man bellowed over the crowd.

*Him.*

I knew it without looking. His voice had enough power to shake my bones, and I scrambled to my feet, turning toward it.

The Alpha.

My head spun.

Lachlan stood at the edge of the ring, his four opponents collapsed behind him. He stared at us, his presence so commanding that I felt it shake me to my core.

I drew in a shuddery breath, unable to look away.

"She killed Danny!" a man to my left shouted.

The Alpha frowned, and the people behind me moved, revealing the body. His brow lowered, his gaze turning thunderous.

"I didn't." My words were too quiet, but he could surely tell what I'd said.

He nodded at someone behind me, and ice shot through me.

A moment later, strong hands gripped my arms. I thrashed, trying to break free, but the grip tightened, and pain flashed. Tears popped to my eyes, but I forced them back.

"Take her to the tower." The Alpha's voice wasn't loud, but it vibrated with such authority that it sent a chill through me.

*The tower.*

Oh, crap. I'd never get out of there.

Guild City had nearly a dozen magical guilds—one for each supernatural species—and those guilds each had a tower. If I went into the shifters' tower, it was over for me.

But hell—I was surrounded by dozens of shifters, including the Alpha. There was no way I was getting out of here, either.

So I let them drag me through the crowd, my mind spinning with escape plans. I didn't know what was about to happen, but I had a dozen schemes thought up, some too wild to even be possible. But I'd always been good with ideas. That would get me out of this.

I clung to the thought. Panic and fear would get me nowhere. I needed to stay calm. Alert.

The guards, two burly men with broad shoulders and thick beards, dragged me up the stairs to the main bar. I didn't know what types of shifters they were. There was a hierarchy, with predators at the top, but it was often impossible to tell when a person was in human form.

It didn't matter.

"You won't get away with it," the shifter on my left muttered.

"You're an idiot if you think I did that."

"Pack won't tolerate it."

"Duh." Of course the pack wouldn't tolerate a murder of one of their own, but his desire to jump in and make the damned statement just pissed me off. Loyalty was their biggest thing, and they flashed it whenever they could.

The night was even colder when they dragged me out into it, and the rain was torrential. It soaked me in seconds, sending cold through my veins.

Across the street and the grassy courtyard beyond, the Shifters' Guild tower loomed. The massive city wall stretched out from either side of the tower, disappearing into the dark, where it would join up with other guild towers.

Guild City itself was roughly circular, surrounded by a wall enchanted to keep us hidden from human London. We were smack in the middle of the city, but not a single human knew we were here—which was how we liked it.

The center of the Guild City was pretty much free territory, full of shops and houses for all supernaturals. The edges, though—those were owned by the guilds. Each resident belonged to a guild, and each guild had a tower set into the wall that acted as their headquarters.

A courtyard sat in front of each tower, and most were bordered by shops owned by that guild.

And I was about to be trapped on the shifters' turf.

I struggled as the guards dragged me across the courtyard and through the massive wooden doors that led into the tower. The main entry room was vaulted, the long rectangular space filled with trestle tables, like something out of an ancient fairytale of knights and ladies. The huge hearth at the far end completed the look. Golden light gleamed from the wooden chandelier overhead, electric now, though it didn't detract from the old castle feeling. Neither did the massive telly mounted to the wall.

The place hadn't changed a bit.

It wouldn't have. Shifters venerated tradition and family, and this place was both. For as long as our pack had been in Guild City, this had been the room where everyone gathered.

They didn't give me a chance to look around, however. Instead, they dragged me toward the back of the room. As we neared the hearth, I had long enough to wonder if they'd take me left or right. Right led to the main living quarters. Left led to the dungeons.

We went left.

I shivered, bone cold.

I had to act.

They'd slowed enough that I'd begun to walk, and I used it to my advantage. I dropped to my knees, letting my weight break their grip. Only one let go, but I managed to kick the other right in the balls.

He howled and fell. I rolled away, reaching for the heavy leather bracelet that I wore around my left wrist. Thin vials of potion were attached to it, and I yanked one free, uncorking it with my thumb.

The shifter that I hadn't kicked lunged for me, and I raised the vial to my face and blew. A cloud of blue smoke wafted into his face. His eyes crossed, and he tumbled with a heavy thud, unconscious.

I jumped over him, stopping just long enough to dump the rest of the blue powder onto the face of the man who still rolled around on the ground, clutching his balls. He fell still and silent.

Heart pounding, I sprinted for the door. I had just minutes—maybe seconds—before the other shifters followed. I had to get the hell off of their turf.

But then what? They'd recognize me if they saw me on the street.

I'd have to leave town.

After everything I'd done in Guild City—everything I'd paid—I would have to leave.

The idea broke my heart. I'd tried to leave before, and I missed the city like a limb. It was the only place I wanted to live.

But the alternative was worse.

I reached the enormous door and yanked it open, ready to sprint out into the night...only to run headfirst into another guard. A grunt escaped me, and he gripped my arms.

Unfortunately, there were six behind him, each bigger than the last. And beyond them, the Alpha, striding across the courtyard toward us.

*Shit.*

I shifted left, out of Lachlan's eyeline, but I was pretty sure his gaze had landed on me. I swallowed hard and looked up at the wide-eyed guard who stared at the bodies behind me.

I wasn't great at math, but it was clear enough that I was *very* outnumbered.

They didn't hesitate.

The two biggest shifters stepped forward and grabbed me by the arms, dragging me backward through the main room. The other guards closed ranks behind them, cutting off my view of Lachlan before our eyes could meet.

These guards were no fools. They dragged me so fast that my heels scraped the ground.

I could take on two, as long as surprise was on my side. I wasn't dumb enough to try it now, though, which meant that I was dragged quickly through the depths of the tower and tossed into one of the damp, dark cells at the bottom. I landed on my butt in the cold dirt and scrambled up with a hiss.

Two female guards approached. Quick as snakes, they stripped off my leather cuff bracelet and searched my pockets, taking my envelope of cash, my mobile, my wallet, and the last of my candy bars.

"Hey! That's mine!" I yelped.

The bigger guard glared. "You're lucky that's all we took."

Horror flashed through me.

My necklace. It had been enchanted with a special potion to turn me into a fae. If I lost it, they'd know I was a shifter. If Lachlan saw me without it, he might even sense I was his mate, since it hid the magical signature that marked me as his.

I shut my mouth and backed up toward the wall.

She nodded and turned to leave, and the other one followed. They slammed the door behind them.

I ran to the small window and clutched the bars, staring at the guards who'd just locked the door. They strode away, not bothering to look back.

Fear shivered through me.

Alone.

Trapped.

No, not entirely alone.

I had friends who could help get me out of this. It had taken me a long time to find another guild after I'd run away from the shifters. Just this year, I'd joined the Shadow Guild. Unlike other guilds, which were species-specific, the Shadow Guild was home to all sorts of supernaturals. It was a guild for the misfits and outcasts.

I fit right in.

But no. I couldn't drag them all the way here and direct the shifters' anger at them. My friends didn't even know what I was. Not a single person in the world besides the blackmailer knew that I was the chosen one of the Shifters' Guild, fated to be the Alpha's mate. My friends believed I was a fae without a court—a terrible fate, to be sure, but not as bad as the truth.

The lies had been getting heavy, and now they felt like they might crush me into the ground. I was an asshole for lying, but I hadn't seen any other way. I tried to be a good friend otherwise, giving all of my adrift shifter loyalty to them—which was exactly why I couldn't drag them into this. I'd never do that to them. I might be innocent of this crime, but I was still guilty of running. Sneaking away in the dead of night without a word to anyone had been the ultimate act of disloyalty to the pack, especially given that I was meant to be the chosen one. Unforgivable.

I shook my head violently, trying to drive away the thoughts. I didn't have time to be circling that emotional drain. I needed to figure out what the hell to do.

More than likely, they'd come to collect me for an audience with the Alpha. He determined the fate of wrongdoers in his pack. And it wasn't like I would have stood a better chance with a jury of my peers. The shifters were loyal, almost blindingly so. They'd caught me with the body and thought I was an outsider.

They'd want blood for that.

I shivered and rubbed my arms.

The idea of facing down Lachlan made me almost sick inside. What if he recognized me?

I couldn't bear it.

My last memory of him was from when he'd learned that I was meant to be his fated mate.

*Her? She's a mutt.*

The words still burned. I couldn't shift, *and* I'd been an ugly duckling. Combined with the seer's prophecy that being his mate would end in my death, his scorn had been the one-two punch that had sent me running.

With my mom recently dead, there was nothing left for me in Guild City. No way was I going to stay and get kicked around by Lachlan or face the mysterious and horrible prophecy laid down by the seer who was never wrong.

Fortunately, my mom had kept some spare cash lying around, and she'd had nice jewelry. As much as I'd hated selling it, the nest egg had built me a little life in London. Not a great one, but a free one. Her friend, a potion master named Liora, had put me up for a while, teaching me everything I needed to know to create a life for myself and hide what I was. It had been an incredible gift, actually, since Liora knew how to fake being a fae. It was magic that should have been impossible, but I'd learned it and used it to make the potion that anointed my necklace.

I'd returned to Guild City when I was twenty, after

I'd learned enough about potions to use them to conceal myself. The fact that I was no longer an ugly duckling helped.

When I'd first left, I'd planned to stay in London, but I'd missed Guild City too badly to stay away. But now I was stuck here.

Heart pounding, I stared at the door.

What the hell was I going to do?

## 3

*Eve*

Sometime later, the door swung open. It jarred me from an uneasy sleep against the wall, and I leapt to my feet.

A stocky guard stood at the entrance, glowering. "He'll see you now."

Cold rushed over me.

*Shit.*

The guard strode forward, reaching out to grab my arm. His grip made my skin crawl, and he tugged me toward him.

I yanked myself free. "I can walk."

He growled, and I got a hit of his magic—the scent of grass and the sound of birds screeching. Each supernatural had a magical signature that corresponded to one or more of the five senses, and the strongest had all five. For shifters, their signatures didn't necessarily correspond to their animal side, but I'd bet money this guy was some kind of bird of prey. But he only had two signatures, so he was of moderate strength.

I could probably take him.

A sound in the hall caught my attention, and I looked around him. Four more guards.

*Double shit.*

"Don't even think of trying anything," he said.

Yeah, I wasn't an idiot.

"Looks like I'm going to meet the Alpha," I said.

"I know." The guard frowned.

"I wasn't talking to you." I strode forward and stepped around him. I didn't like my fate, but I wasn't going to cower.

As the guards escorted me up the wide stone stairs, fear iced me to my bones. Years of hiding had made me exceptionally wary, and my self-preservation instincts were in overdrive.

What if he recognized me?

Surreptitiously, I touched my pointed ears. He'd buy it. As far as he knew, it was impossible to fake your species. And anyway, I looked so different now.

All the same, terror followed me every step of the way.

As we climbed to the main level, I caught the sounds of conversation and music. Shifters loved to party.

Normally, I loved a good party. Now? It was just more of an unwanted audience.

Stepping into to the main room, I straightened my shoulders and stiffened my spine. No way I was going to let them see how scared I was.

"Go on." The guard nudged me, and I walked forward.

The room I'd passed through earlier looked entirely different now, full of people and food and a band in the corner—it really was a party. It seemed like it'd been going for hours, with cups and plates everywhere.

Homesickness pierced me.

Sure, I still lived in Guild City, and I would never leave. But this part of it—the shifters' domain—had been my first home, and I missed it.

Anger heated my blood, giving me strength.

Good thing, too, because I caught sight of Lachlan then.

I'd seen him a few times on the street and ducked my head, but this was *entirely* different. He sat in the massive wooden chair by the fire, relaxed yet deadly. His massive form was draped gracefully, arms over the armrests and one ankle propped on a knee. He looked like the king he was—a warrior king. Sweaty and bruised from battle, he was a beauty, though a brutal one. The golden firelight flickered over his dark hair, making his green eyes look like shadowed emeralds as he studied me.

There was an eerie stillness about him, the kind that marked true predators. As the Alpha Wolf, he was the truest predator of them all. This post wasn't his by gift of his father—he'd earned it.

I swallowed hard and strode up to him, stopping ten feet from the chair. *Throne*, more like.

Even from this distance, his magical signatures hit me in the face. The scent of evergreen, the sound of a low growl, the taste of whiskey, and the feeling of a strong embrace. Protective. Or destructive, depending.

He was a man of contrasts, particularly his aura. Only the strongest supernaturals had auras, and his was wild. He was a core of fire surrounded by ice. Tightly leashed power, yet something inside him desperately wanted to be let free.

His wolf?

There was something...*broken* about him. But it also seemed like he'd welded himself back together, made himself stronger, somehow. Fucked up, but stronger.

My gaze finally met his, and a connection zipped between us, a zing of energy that crossed the air. Almost like my soul recognized him, and it scared the shit out of me.

He arched a dark brow. "Looked your fill?"

Like many of the shifters in this pack, his accent was Scottish. Our ancestral grounds were there, and he'd spent a lot of time in the Highlands as a child. I fought back a blush. "Not much to look at."

The words had been waiting a decade to come out, and damn, did they feel good.

The fact that they were a lie was beside the point.

The corner of his mouth twitched slightly, almost like he would smile. I found myself riveted by his mouth, far more interested than I should be.

He frowned, instead, then surged to his feet.

He was utterly massive, like a redwood built of muscle. The T-shirt that stretched across his shoulders was threadbare, as if it fought every day of its dumb life to hang on to him. If he hadn't been such a bastard to me all those years ago, I might have wanted to hang on to him, too.

As it was, he'd been horrid, and I hated him.

The fact that he looked nothing like the boy I once knew didn't matter. It didn't matter that it seemed like the weight of the world now rested on his shoulders.

Fear shivered through me as he approached.

Tension tightened the air between us, sending heat through me. I breathed shallowly, trying to get a hold of myself. The connection between us now felt more like an invisible wire, drawing us together by forces I didn't understand. My entire body was lit up like I'd eaten fairy lights.

What was this feeling?

His gaze traveled over me. Did he feel it, too? Did he recognize me?

He frowned again as he looked me up and down, his gaze lingering on my magically enhanced pointed ears.

*Look all you like, buddy. They're not going anywhere.*

Unless he took my necklace off.

He glanced over my head at the party going on behind me and nodded. The music abruptly cut off, and I didn't need to turn around to know that people were quickly clearing out.

His word was law here.

"You're Eve. No last name."

"I don't have one."

"Hmm. You're the potion maker from town." He walked a circle around me, like a predator inspecting its prey. Every inch of me was wound so tightly, I could have snapped.

Did he *really* not recognize me? He hadn't said anything yet.

His voice was a low rumble from behind me. "You killed Danny."

"Are you fucking serious?" I spun to face him, knowing that one didn't curse at the Alpha. I didn't care, especially if he didn't recognize me. "We were in the middle of Pandemonium, for fates' sake, and you think I decided to murder him right there with a fast-acting potion?"

"You're good with potions, aren't you?"

My temper surged. "Good enough to know the difference between fast-acting and slow and not to mess it up. You have some of my things, by the way. I'd like them back."

"Maybe." He gave me a long look, clearly searching for something.

His gaze sent a rush of nervous heat over me, as if my body didn't know how to react to him. I *hated* it.

He stepped up to me, his evergreen scent wrapping around me. I breathed shallowly through my mouth, determined to like nothing about him. He stopped two feet from me, and every hair on my body stood on end.

"Why are you hiding your signature?" he murmured. "Your scent is off."

*Shit.*

It was possible for powerful supernaturals to repress some of their magical signature, and he was right—I was doing just that. My natural signature was so unusual that it risked giving me away.

I shrugged. "I'm just not that powerful. It's why I focus on potions. Making up for my shortcomings."

"I sincerely doubt that." His voice purred over my skin, threatening yet sexy.

I fucking hated him.

I fucking hated myself for wanting him.

"Well, it's true." I crossed my arms.

"It's all very suspicious, don't you think?" he asked. "You're hiding something about your magic, and you came here with a bracelet full of potions and an envelope full of cash. You used one of those potions to knock out my guards."

I swallowed hard. "I always wear the bracelet. It's not like I put it on so I could use it against your pack."

He gave a low laugh. "And you've got nothing to say about the money?"

"Coincidence."

"Was it for Danny?"

"No."

"I'm not sure I believe you. Why shouldn't I just toss you back in that dungeon right now?"

My heart raced. "That isn't fair. I deserve a trial. Guild City has rules."

"Not rules that touch us."

Damn it, he was right.

The Council of Guilds served as the central government for Guild City, and though the shifters technically sat on the council, they were subject to different rules. The pack—and the Alpha—would never consent to being ruled by outsiders. They ran according to their own laws, and things were different here. You could feel it in the air as you stepped onto their turf.

*We are not like the others.*

It might as well have been their motto. Instead, it was *Urram, Misneachd, Dìlseachd*, Scots Gaelic for *Honor, Courage, Loyalty*.

Which meant that I was on my own.

My heart raced, fear propelling me. "I *didn't* do it. Let

me prove I'm innocent, because locking me up won't help if the killer plans to do it again."

"How are you qualified to solve a murder?"

My mind raced. "I'm an excellent potion maker. I can analyze the poison that killed him. And I'm friends with Carrow Burton, leader of the Shadow Guild and the city's number one sleuth. She solves crimes for a living."

"I know of her."

"Then you know she's good. And so am I. Best potion maker in town. Give me a chance, and I'll prove my innocence." It was my only hope.

He studied me for a long moment, and it felt like he could see straight into my soul.

My mind raced as I tried to come up with reasons for him to let me go. If I could prove my innocence, maybe I could even get my money back. "The potion that killed Danny is one of your best clues, and I can help identify it and maybe lead us to the killer. You need me."

"Maybe." He walked around me, back toward his throne, and I turned to watch him go. He picked up a circle of golden metal that I hadn't noticed slung over the chair arm and returned to me.

His stride was relentless, and in seconds, he was right in front of me, so close that I could smell him. Earthy and dark, the sweat of the fight wasn't a bad smell. No, I *liked* it.

"You can prove your innocence," he said, "but you'll wear this." He moved so quickly that I didn't see it coming. One moment, I was standing there, totally normal, and the next, I was wearing a golden collar around my neck.

"What the hell?" I reached up for it, trying to yank it off. The damned thing didn't budge. Anger seethed through me.

A *collar*. That bastard had put a collar on me. Like a *dog*.

Old anger and hurt surged to the surface.

I'd never wanted to hex anyone so badly in my entire life, and I wasn't even a witch. When this was over, I was going straight to the Witches' Guild to learn how to hex his balls off.

"It's just a tracking collar," he said. "Nothing dangerous."

Not dangerous until he decided to come find me and kill me if I didn't solve this murder quickly enough. I grimaced and lowered my hand. "You're a bastard."

He nodded, his gaze flashing with the heat and ice that I'd seen in his aura. "As long as you understand that, we're good. Don't try to run, because I will find you. Don't try to take it off, because you can't. Until you prove your innocence, you're mine."

*You're mine.*

# 4

*Lachlan*

I stared at the woman, unable to take my eyes off her.

She was so beautiful and...*bright.*

Looking at her was like looking at the moon, and the beast inside me liked it. Too much.

I clenched a fist, trying to drive the feeling back. I'd only had this sensation once before, when I'd seen the girl that fate had chosen for me. I'd lashed out then, knowing that I couldn't afford any kind of feeling like that. I still couldn't afford it. Not for anyone.

But her scent...

It wrapped around me like silk, drawing me to her. It took everything I had to keep my distance. To rein in my wolf, that most bestial part of me that acted on instinct and desire.

I reached into my pocket and pulled out the steel flask, taking a swig of the whisky that never gave me a buzz. My metabolism was too fast. But I liked the burn, along with the potion laced with the alcohol. The damned potion that kept stronger emotions at bay. Emotions were a bane for some of my kind—for my line in particular—driving us to the madness of the Dark Moon curse.

She eyed my flask and raised a brow. "Isn't it a little early for that?"

"No."

"It's almost morning."

"Then it's still late at night."

The collar glinted around her neck, and I wondered if letting her help was madness.

No. I wanted to know what she was up to. I'd tried to wind her up with my threats of throwing her in our dungeon, and she'd stayed cool.

I was almost certain she hadn't killed Danny. We'd found a few witness statements that I trusted, and she'd barely held his glass at all—not long enough to slip a potion in. To add to it, we'd analyzed the potions in her cuff, and none had been even close to poison.

But she was up to something, coming onto our turf with enough cash to buy a nice car. No one walked around with money like that. And her hidden signature…

She was a mystery, and I wanted answers.

"I need to see the body," she said.

I nodded. "I'll show you."

"And I need my things back."

Again, I nodded. "Come on, then."

She hurried to keep up, walking beside me through the main room. I couldn't keep my traitorous eyes off her. Her silver and pink hair glinted under the light, riveting. Oddly enough, she was almost familiar. Like the girl I'd once known, so briefly. But that girl had been a wolf, and this one was fae. And she looked entirely different.

That girl was gone, and good riddance. She'd disappeared in the dead of night, not leaving a trace. I'd tried to drive her off, and it had worked. My cruel words still sent a little shaft of guilt through me, but they'd been necessary. And they'd worked. She'd run.

She hadn't needed to be so careful hiding her tracks, though. I wouldn't hunt her.

No matter how much I might want to.

I couldn't.

I also couldn't afford to think of her right now. Danny had been a weasel of a pack member, but he'd been one of my brother's friends. One of my last links to Garreth.

I drove the thought away, considering another pull

from my flask. Instead, I quickened my pace. She kept up, and I led her through the twisting hallways of the guild tower toward my quarters. When we reached them, I stopped at the door. "You'll wait here."

"Fine."

I let myself inside the sparse, austere rooms and went over to the table by the hearth. Her wallet, cuff, mobile, and envelope of cash sat there. I picked up everything but the cash and returned to her, handing them over.

She frowned. "Where's the money? And all the potions are gone from my cuff. And my chocolates aren't here."

"We had to test the potions and chocolates. They're gone. You'll get the money back when this is all over." *And once I've figured out what you're hiding.*

She scowled at me but didn't fight. "Just take me to the body."

"This way." I led her down to the main level of the tower, cutting toward the back of the building. "The body is in the meat freezer," I said, pushing open the door to the massive kitchen.

"What the hell?"

"We're not in the habit of having murder victims in the pack. We don't have the facilities."

"You could have taken him to the morgue."

"Outside our turf? Never."

"So you put him where you put the food."

"Aye." I reached the huge metal door and pulled it open, reveling in the icy air that flowed out. "And he's not touching any of the food."

"Still, gross." She slipped in before me, and I inhaled her scent as she passed, unable to help myself. I tilted my head back and squeezed my eyes closed, trying to get control of myself.

It was fine to want her. It'd been years, after all. But it wasn't fine to act on it.

Again, I wanted to reach for my flask, but I resisted. Self-control was a game I played—one of the only games.

She stopped beside Danny's body, which had been laid out on the massive table in the middle. "Did you search the corpse?" she asked.

"Aye." I pulled a business card out of my pocket. "Besides his wallet and cigarettes, this was all we found on him."

I handed it to her, and she studied it, something flashing in her eyes. Worry? "Clarence Tomes. I don't recognize it."

"How did you know Danny?" I asked. "I've never seen you around him."

"Don't really know him. He stopped me and asked me to hold his drink while he got a cigarette."

"No smoking in Pandemonium."

"That's what I told him." She turned back to the body, inspecting Danny's face.

I stepped up beside her to get a better look, trying to ignore what it felt like to be around her. It was almost like my heart moved more quickly, my mind was more engaged.

She was a curiosity, that was all. I'd been alone too long—not that that was going to change—and she was a distraction. Yet the pull I felt toward her...that wasn't normal.

I needed to be careful around her. I couldn't afford a distraction, especially not from a pretty fae.

She leaned closer to the body, her gaze on his face. Dark veins had appeared beneath Danny's skin, and his eyes had swollen closed. "Do you recognize what's happened to him?" I asked.

She frowned. "There's a couple things it could be. Do you have the glass he was drinking from?"

"It's at the scene, which has been locked down."

"I need to get that glass. Can I speak to the bartender who was on last night, too?"

I nodded. "Aye. Follow me."

Together, we walked through the tower. People moved aside and inclined their heads as I passed, and I felt the fae watching me. She said nothing, though, and it was for the best.

I led the way from the tower. The sun was rising over the city walls as we crossed the courtyard to Pandemonium, and I looked down at Eve. "Clara, the bartender, lives above the place."

She nodded. "She's going to hate me knocking at this hour."

"She'll do as her Alpha commands."

Eve grimaced.

"Do you have a problem with our way of life?"

"I don't know anything about it."

We'd reached the front of Pandemonium. I pointed to the small dormer windows at the third story. "She lives there. We can go around the side."

She nodded. "I've got it from here. No need to have the Alpha accompanying me."

"I'm coming."

She glowered at me. "Suit yourself."

I led her to an alley between Pandemonium and the shop next door. The narrow space was cobblestoned and damp, smelling faintly of vomit. They were over-serving at Pandemonium, no doubt. I used the club for the monthly fights—the one release I allowed my wolf, besides runs in the Highlands—but never drank there. "Here." I stopped by a narrow green door and pushed it open, then climbed the steps to the third floor.

Eve followed closely, stopping just behind me and watching as I knocked on the door. From within, a thump sounded, as if someone were falling out of bed. Footsteps followed, and I could smell the distinct signature of Clara, cloves and orange.

A moment later, she pulled open the door and stared out at us groggily. Clara's purple hair stuck out at all angles, matching the shadows under her eyes. The annoyance on her face transformed to respect when she saw me, and she straightened as she lowered her gaze. "Alpha. How can I help you?"

"Clara. You can answer her questions." I nodded to Eve.

Clara looked at Eve, her gaze flashing with confusion. "Okay."

"Yes," Eve said. "I have a few questions about Danny."

"Really? I thought you were here to ask about my stylist." Her tone was sarcastic as she patted her hair.

"Clara."

She perked at the warning tone in my voice. "Apologies. What can I do?"

"Did you serve Danny last night?" Eve asked.

"He didn't get the drink from us."

"Really?"

"Really. Someone else must have ordered for him."

"And you didn't see who did?" Eve pressed.

"No. But Danny liked whisky, and he wouldn't turn down a free drink."

"He would have been an easy mark."

She nodded. "Probably, but I didn't see who did it. I thought it was you."

"But you served me a beer."

She frowned. "You're right. Doesn't mean you couldn't have brought whisky in a flask and poured it into an empty glass you found. Or dropped a bit of potion in the glass he handed you."

Clara was clever. We'd found no flask on Eve, however, and she hadn't held the glass long enough to slip anything into it. Probably.

"Well, I didn't," Eve said. "You haven't been down to the bar since the incident?"

"No, it's on lockdown. Alpha's orders."

"Thank you." Eve turned to me. "We need to go get that broken glass."

"I have the key."

"Thanks." Eve turned back to Clara. "Was there anyone in the bar last night that you didn't recognize?"

I studied Eve, wondering what her deal was. She was determined to solve this, but why had she been there in the first place?

"I didn't recognize you," Clara said. "And a few others."

"Can you describe them?" Eve asked.

"An artist is coming by to help you do that later," I told Clara.

She nodded. "I'll work with them."

"Good." Eve looked satisfied.

"Thank you for your help," I said. "We're going to go check the bar."

"Let me know if there's anything I can do to help." Clara frowned. "I didn't like Danny, but he was pack. What happened to him was wrong."

"It'd be wrong even if he weren't pack," Eve said.

"Sure. It's just worse."

Eve ignored that and turned to go. I followed her down the stairs, my gaze on her bright hair. It gleamed under the light, and occasionally, I caught sight of one of her pointed fae ears.

I looked away.

We reached the street and headed out into the alley. Pandemonium was dark and quiet as I let us in. I led the way down the stairs to the basement, then flicked on a light. It looked dingier without people filling it, but I preferred the quiet. Empty beer bottles and glasses were scattered all over the tables, and the floor was still sticky.

Eve headed straight for the shattered glass near the wall. She knelt and peered down at it, then rose and went to the bar, where she collected a half-spent kitchen roll. "I'm going to take some of this, all right?" she said.

"Aye."

I met her at the broken glass and knelt down to inspect the pieces. She joined me, kneeling as far away from me as she could but still so close that I wanted to move aside.

She picked up a piece of glass with the towel and turned it over under the light. A bit of liquid had dried inside the glass, sticking to the side with an oily sheen.

"That will be the potion that killed him," she said. "Left behind after the whisky evaporated."

Carefully, she collected and wrapped the shards.

When she was done, she stood. "I'll need to take that back to my workshop to—"

"You'll do it here."

"I really can't." She pointed to the collar, glaring at me. "And it's not like you're going to lose track of me."

She was right. It was just that I didn't want to let her out of my sight.

It was fucked up. There was no reason to be attached to her. No reason to be attached to anything other than my pack.

Some distance would be good. I needed to get my head on straight where she was concerned, because none of this made sense.

"Fine. You may go. But you'll report back this evening," I said.

She nodded. "And you'll look for the person on the business card? And get sketches of the other people made?"

"Of course."

"I'll be back tonight to report on what I find. Leave me alone until then." She spun and strode out of the bar.

I watched her go, her hips swaying as she strode away. I turned toward the fight ring, needing to focus on something other than her curves. I'd avoided women for years now—ever since I'd been eighteen and my father had fallen prey to the Dark Moon curse. Ever since *she'd* left.

All shifters were at risk for the curse, but my line particularly so. Too much emotion—especially strong emotion—and we would succumb to a madness that would steal our loyalty to our pack and eventually our minds. We'd go feral, our wolves taking over.

It had taken my father, but it would not take me.

I wouldn't let it.

Quickly, I took a swig of the potion-laced whiskey, counting on it to help repress any emotions that might try to sneak through. I needed to be the cunning, clear-headed Alpha that I always was.

The fae woman was a problem, but it was possible she wasn't Danny's killer.

She was hiding something, however, and I was determined to get to the bottom of it.

**5**

---

*Eve*

I raced from the bar, hurrying up the stairs and out into the cool morning air. The sun was just starting to peek over the horizon, and I used its faint light to beeline it out of the shifters' territory and into the main part of Guild City.

As I strode away from the tower, I turned back to look across the grassy courtyard. Lachlan was nowhere to be seen, but the hulking tower speared toward the sky.

*I can't believe I was just inside the shifters' tower.*

I shuddered and turned away, heading toward town.

As I stepped into neutral turf, I reached up to tug on

the collar. The damned thing wouldn't budge. Worse, I could feel the magic buzzing around it.

Lachlan could find me anytime.

I shivered.

Had he really not recognized me?

I'd felt his gaze on me frequently, especially on my pointed ears. It had felt both curious and almost...angry. But he hadn't seemed to recognize me. Thank fates I looked entirely different, but it had to be the species change that convinced him. As far as most supernaturals knew, it was impossible to change species. Sure, a glamour could make me look fae, but I shouldn't be able to fake the magic. I could, though. Not only did I have a magical signature that was vaguely fae, I could throw lightning, grow plants, and even fly. I'd need to find a reason to use my wings around him, just to throw him off the scent.

"Hey! Watch where you're going!" A man dodged out of my way, glowering at me.

"Sorry!" I'd totally lost track of my surroundings, and the city streets were busier than I'd realized.

*Not good.*

I was still reeling from seeing Lachlan. He was so different—so powerful, yet so contained. Like a massive stone island in the middle of a sea storm.

And the connection between us...what the hell was that?

I dragged my thoughts from Lachlan so that I could

avoid knocking into anyone. Guild City didn't have room for cars on the ancient, narrow streets, but there were hundreds of motorbikes. They buzzed by as I hurried along the pavement, passing in front of the ancient façades of the Tudor buildings. The exteriors of the buildings hadn't changed much since the city was built five hundred years ago. They were still the same dark wood and white plaster, with many of the original diamond-pane windows—all except for the shops, which had large glass fronts to display their wares.

I passed in front of them, the windows glittering invitingly. Clothing, electronics, weapons, spells, house-wares, stationery—everything was for sale on this street, and most of it danced inside the windows, propelled by magic to invite the customer to take a closer look.

Before, I'd been perpetually skint due to Danny. Maybe now, if I could solve this and get my money back, I'd have some breathing room.

*I'm free.*

Almost.

Guilt stabbed me. Danny had been an utter bastard, but he hadn't deserved to die like that.

My thoughts trailed back to Lachlan. He hadn't recognized me yet, and maybe he never would. If he didn't, then my secret died with Danny.

It didn't take long to cut across town and make my way to the Shadow Guild tower, where I lived and worked. As I walked, I rolled through what I knew of Danny:

1. He had been scared to leave shifter turf.

2. Before he'd died, he said something about a bastard finally...doing something.

3. He was a blackmailer.

Had one of his other victims killed him? Surely not the person whose business card he'd been holding...

I couldn't rule it out, but that would be too easy. Nothing in my life was that easy.

The sun was fully overhead when I arrived, shining on the tall, slender stone tower that acted as the Shadow Guild's headquarters. It wasn't nearly as big as the shifters' tower, but then there weren't nearly as many of us, only half a dozen of Guild City's misfits.

Though it wasn't big, our tower was far more beautiful. The stone gleamed a pale gray that almost sparkled under the sunlight. The glass windows *definitely* sparkled, so brightly that the diamond-shaped panes looked like precious gems themselves. Roses climbed up the side walls, courtesy of my fake fae earth magic.

Guilt pierced me again. My friends knew that I was an accomplished potion maker. They didn't know that I was so good I could fake my species.

I shook away the guilt and hurried toward the tower. I loved living in such an ancient-looking place with all the conveniences of modern living. Guild City was perfect for that, and our fairytale tower was the crown jewel.

I let myself in the front door and calling out, "Hello? Anyone in?"

Fortunately, no one answered me. I wasn't ready to face questions yet.

I'd only just moved into the Shadow Guild tower, while the others still lived in their flats. They hung out here often, though, as we used it for meetings and parties.

Until recently, I'd had two workshops out in Guild City: my main business, which I'd moved here in order to save money so I could pay off Danny, and a secret workshop hidden across town. The hidden one was just a hidey hole where I made the potion that changed my species. I had to regularly create the potion that I dipped my necklace in, and I didn't want to store the extremely rare ingredients in a place that could be robbed.

I took the stairs two at a time to my workshop and private flat. As I let myself into my new home, I gave a sigh of relief and leaned against the door. The little living room was filled with plush, colorful furniture and old art that I'd scavenged years ago from car boot sales out in London. Everything looked just as I'd left it.

"Thank fates." Though I'd only moved into the flat recently, it felt like home.

I set the bundle of towels and glass on the table by the door. Before I could deal with that, I needed a chocolate bar and a damned shower. I was so tense that a million chocolate bars wouldn't fix me, but I could sure as hell try. I went to the tiny kitchen and opened one of the drawers where I kept my stash.

It was empty.

I scowled down at it. It had been full just yesterday…

I looked up toward the window. A furry face stared at me through the glass, its black eyes glinting with fiendish delight. They were surrounded by a black mask and gray fur.

Goddamned raccoon. I should have known.

Raccoons weren't even supposed to *live* in London, and yet, one had found its way to me and seemed to have dedicated its life to stealing my damned chocolate bars. Our friend and guild leader, Carrow Burton, had a raccoon named Cordelia as a familiar. But this one was different. Cordelia was a sneak, but this one was an outright thief.

Guild City was positively infested.

I'd even taken to leaving out healthy snacks for the little wanker, feeling a bit bad for the creature and hoping to keep him off my stash. He'd completely ignored the offering and had been waging a campaign of terror against me ever since, sneaking into every hiding spot.

"I will get you," I said to the furry little bandit. "Just you wait."

He grinned and ducked down, disappearing.

On my way to the shower, I grabbed a Lion bar that I'd taped under a lampshade and shoved half of it into my mouth. This was what he'd reduced me to—hiding chocolate everywhere like a lunatic.

I made quick work of my shower, then returned to the bedroom.

My closet was a mess, but it didn't take long to discard the idea of putting on one of the flowy dresses I liked. Things were looking dangerous, and that called for jeans and leather. I changed as quickly as I could, then returned to the living room and gathered up the little bundle of broken glass.

My workshop was just across the hall, and stepping inside felt like walking into a therapist's office. *Here* was where I made sense of things, where I gained clarity and control.

I looked down at the bundle of glass. "I'm going to find who made you."

First things first—I needed one of Liora's books. She'd given me several when I'd left, along with some of her most valuable supplies, and they were my prized possession. They made me one of the best potion masters in the world, and that had changed my life. It had given me the freedom I needed to keep living in the city I loved.

I set to work gathering ingredients and lighting a tiny magical fire under a little silver cauldron. This was precision work, not quantity work.

My mind went blessedly blank as I began to measure out the ingredients into the little pot. When it was all bubbling and fragrant, I picked up one of the broken pieces of glass and made sure it had an oily sheen on the inside.

"You're mine, you bastard." I dropped it into the potion and grabbed the book, waiting for the liquid to start smoking. Within a minute, a sparkling green mist unfurled from the top of the liquid. It shimmered with an almost oily texture. Quickly, I flipped through the book, which was indexed by smoke color, and finally found a match.

"The Ageratina potion?"

"The Agerawhat?" My friend Mac's voice sounded from the door, and I jerked my head out of the book.

MacBeth O'Connell stood in the doorway, her jeans ragged at the knees and tucked into black leather motorcycle boots. She wore a plaid shirt open to reveal a tank top, while her short blond hair was messy around her head. She was tall and slender, and as usual, looked like a female hipster lumberjack. A hot one.

It was a weird look, but it worked on her.

"Mac. What's up?" My heartbeat thundered in my ears. I wanted to see her—I loved Mac—but I was right in the middle of my own personal secret hellscape.

"Not much. I think I should be asking you that." She pointed to the smoke. "What's going on there?"

My mind spun. What the hell to tell her?

Part of me wanted to confess. Desperately.

I played with my necklace, a horrible nervous tic whenever I thought about my lies.

She would keep my secret. I loved Mac, and she loved me. But I'd never told her, and now it had been years. At first, I hadn't trusted anyone. I'd been on the run for so long that I didn't know how. And now the secret had slipped out of control.

I reached for a partially unwrapped chocolate bar that sat on the counter between a few bottles of potions and chewed, not caring that it had been sitting open for weeks, most likely.

"Stress chocolate?" Mac asked. "What's wrong?" She walked forward, frowning at my neck. "What the heck is that?"

I touched it, chewing frantically and debating another bite. "Um...it's a collar."

"What kind?" Her tone was wary as she stopped in front of me and held her hand in front of my neck. "I can feel the magic inside."

"Yeah. About that..." I hesitated for half a second, then let it all spill out. Not my past or my true species, but the murder and everything. The Alpha. The deadline to prove my innocence.

When I was done, she rocked back on her heels, her face pale. "So the shifters want you for murder."

I nodded. "It's bad."

"Really bad. They're a law unto themselves. The

Council of Guilds can't step in and make sure that they follow the rules. No one can touch them."

"I know." I shivered.

"Don't worry. We'll get you out of this."

"It's too risky for you to get involved."

"What the hell else are we supposed to do? We're not going to sit around and let you go down for this."

My heart seemed to swell inside my chest. "You guys are the best."

"Well, I won't disagree there." She looked at the green smoke that still spilled out of the cauldron. "Are you working on solving the mystery now?"

I nodded. "That's the Ageratina potion. It was used to kill Danny."

"And now you want to find who made it and get them to tell you who they sold it to."

"Man, you're good at this."

"I *am* a seer, you know." She grinned. "Also, it was obvious."

"I may need help finding the potion maker." I dug into my pocket and pulled out my mobile. "It's a difficult potion to make, but I think there are at least a few people capable. I'm going to text a friend who might know."

Quickly, I typed out a message to Liora, hit *send*, then looked up at Mac.

"Why were you at Pandemonium?" she asked. "I've never known you to want to hit up a fight club."

I said the first thing that came to mind. "A date."

Her eyebrows rose. "You're having me on. You haven't gone on a date in years."

I was an idiot to think she'd believe me. "Yeah, well. It was time. But I never met him. Danny was murdered before it happened."

"Uh-huh." She nodded, clearly suspicious.

"Think what you like. By the way, have you seen a raccoon besides Cordelia hanging around?" I wanted to know, but I also wanted to distract her.

"No. They shouldn't even live in England. Now we've got two?"

"Yeah. I think Cordelia might have a boyfriend. He keeps stealing my sweets. I've even left food out for him but he ignores it and goes straight for my stash."

"Little bastard."

"My thoughts exactly." On the table, my mobile buzzed. I grabbed it and looked at the screen. "It's my friend."

Liora had written a list of four names, but she didn't know where any of them lived.

Shit.

That would take a while to track down. And four was a lot. I looked up at Mac. "We need to narrow this down further. Can you try?"

"I can try, but no promises. You know I'm better at reading people."

"I just need to know who made it."

She nodded and held out a hand. I gave her a piece of the broken glass, and she closed her eyes, focusing. Her magic flared on the air, bringing with it the scent of a misty morning by a river. A moment later, she opened her eyes. "I'm getting nothing. We need to try Carrow."

I nodded. Our friend wasn't a seer, exactly, but she did have a skill for picking up images from objects. She'd turned the skill into a career as a magical PI of sorts, and it would be good to have her input on this, anyway. "Where is she?"

"The Haunted Hound. Quinn is working, and she had something to drop off with him."

The Haunted Hound was the pub where Mac and our friend Quinn worked. It was also one of the portals to human London.

"I've just got to do one thing." I went to the side table where I kept my premade stash of potion vials and refilled my cuff with a bit of everything I might need. "Right, done. Let's go." I grabbed my jacket and shrugged into it, then stuck my mobile in my pocket and picked up one of the shards of glass, wrapping it carefully in a piece of kitchen roll. The rest I left behind, knowing they would be safe here.

Together, Mac and I cut through town to reach the gate that led to the Haunted Hound. There were several gates that led in and out of Guild City, each one enchanted to carry us out of our protected magical zone and into regular London.

The gate itself was a massive stone structure with two tunnels passing through it, a larger one for cargo and a smaller one for people. We headed into the smaller one and through a door at the very end, stepping right into the ether, an ephemeral substance that connected everything on earth. The ether whisked us through space and spat us out in the back hallway of a quiet old pub. My head spun as I recovered. The sound of chatting and the clinking of glasses welcomed us.

I turned and followed Mac out into the main part of the pub. It was a cheery space with a low wooden ceiling and a roaring fire on one side. A ghostly dog slept by the hearth and had done so for as long as I could remember. Small, round tables crowded the pub, but only a few were occupied.

Mac and I turned toward the bar, a long, gleaming wooden surface that separated us from Quinn, our leopard shifter friend. My *only* shifter friend, in fact. He was a broad, handsome man with auburn hair and a ready smile. Thankfully, I'd never known him as a kid.

Sitting at the bar in front of him were Carrow and Seraphia, two of my closest friends.

*To whom I also lie.*

The ugly little thought popped into my mind, but I shoved it back and approached. Carrow's golden hair waved down her back, while Seraphia's dark tresses were tied up with dark green vines that she must have grown herself. Though we knew her as Seraphia, she was technically Persephone, of the goddess fame.

Quinn grinned widely at us as we approached. "What can I get you ladies? Beer? Tea?"

"Tea. Thanks, Quinn." I smiled at him, so grateful to be seeing my friends after my too-long stint in the shifters' jail.

Carrow and Seraphia spun around on their bar stools, their wide grins fading as they took in the collar around my neck. Any hope that they might think it was jewelry fled on the wind.

"What the hell is that?" Carrow asked.

"So...not great news." I drew in a breath and laid out the whole story just as I'd told Mac.

My friends turned whiter as I spoke, and the whole situation made me want to crawl under the bar and hide. I'd really got myself into a mess this time.

When I finished speaking, Carrow held out her hand. "Give it here, then."

"Thanks." I pulled the glass shard from my pocket and handed it over.

She closed her eyes and wrapped a hand loosely around the glass. A few moments passed, and I waited, strung so tense that I felt like I could break.

This had to work, because if it didn't, I was out of leads.

**6**

---

*Eve*

A few moments later, Carrow opened her eyes. "No luck so far, even though I've become better at finding specific information from objects. Did you say you had some possible names? That might help me narrow it down."

"Yeah. I've got them." I pulled out my mobile and read off the list of names that Liora had given me. One of them was just called "the apothecary." Seraphia made an interested noise when I read that one, and I looked at her.

"It's nothing," she said. "I knew someone called the apothecary, but there have to be loads of people in your business with that title."

"Maybe," I said. But a lead was a lead, and Seraphia might be able to help.

"Let me see if I can narrow it down," Carrow said.

Quinn delivered the tea, and I nodded gratefully at him, unable to drink anything until I heard if Carrow was going to be successful. Minutes passed, and I desperately wanted a damned chocolate bar. A third—fourth?—would make me sick, though, so I held off. Barely.

Finally, Carrow opened her eyes. "I saw a woman with a starburst tattoo on the outer corner of her eye. She was really pretty. Straight dark hair pulled up in a ponytail."

"Starburst tattoo." Seraphia grinned. "And dark hair. That *is* the apothecary I know. She's called Alia."

Excitement burst within me. "Do you know where she lives?"

"No. She used to live in the Underworld, but she left." She pulled her mobile out and began to tap away. "Let me see if I can find her."

"Are you texting Hades?" Mac asked, her brows raised.

"No." Seraphia laughed and waved a hand. "He would *never* own a mobile. Wouldn't even know what to do with one. Probably just throw it at a demon. I'm texting Lucifer."

"Lucifer?" I asked. "As in, *the*?" And why the heck would Satan have a mobile if Hades wouldn't?

"The one and only. He used to have a major thing for Alia when she lived in the Underworld. If anyone would know where she is, it's him."

"Thank you." Gratitude welled within me. Having friends like these made all the difference.

A few moments later, her mobile buzzed. She picked it up and looked down. "Apparently, she now works for Damian Malek in Magic Side, Chicago."

"Damian Malek?" Carrow frowned. "The fallen angel? He's basically a mob boss over there."

"Do you know him?" I asked.

"Not really. Met him once at a casino in Monte Carlo, when he was using an alias. He knows Grey."

Grey, aka the Devil of Darkvale, was Carrow's partner. He was the most powerful vampire in Guild City, and something of a mob boss himself.

"If the Devil knows Damian, then can he get us in to see Alia?"

"Yeah, should be able to." Carrow pulled out her mobile. "Let me check."

"Thank you so much." I looked at the clock over the bar and realized that it was already five p.m. "Where the hell did the day go?"

"It's not even dinnertime," Carrow said.

I touched my collar. "Yeah, but I'm supposed to go back to the Shifters' Guild tower to check in."

She frowned. "This is unacceptable. He can't do that to you."

"The thing is, he can." As much as I hated to admit it, Lachlan *did* have that power. Carrow was still relatively new to magical life, and though she knew loads, little things like that could still escape her. "No one would dare go up against him."

"Grey would," Carrow said.

She was right. If she asked him, he would. The Devil of Darkvale was the most powerful man in Guild City besides Lachlan. But the fight that would result from that...

I couldn't bear to think of it.

"You know it would be a disaster," I said. "Let me see if I can get myself out of this."

"Fine. For now. But we're going to make sure nothing happens to you," Carrow said. "Don't worry. I'll get Grey to hook us up with a meeting."

"Thank you, you're the best."

"I know. But so are you."

"We can't both be."

"Break up the love fest, you two," Mac said. "You're both great, we're all great, but we need to get to work."

I shot her a grateful look, then glanced toward the hallway that led to Guild City. "I need to get back. I'll call you when I know my next steps."

"Be careful," Carrow said.

"Of course."

The thing was, I didn't know how far *careful* was going to get me when the shifters were out for my head.

. . .

***

*Lachlan*

My quarters were blissfully silent as I stared into the fire. The flames were meditative, working almost as well as the whisky to keep my thoughts at bay. Thoughts of her.

Why should a fae intrigue me so?

What I felt with her...it was almost like the mate bond I'd felt so briefly with the girl so long ago. Yet it couldn't be. It just wasn't rational.

I pushed her from my mind. Finding my packmate's killer should be my top goal.

And finding out what the hell the fae was up to.

A knock sounded at the door, and I rose to answer it. "Come in."

The heavy wooden door swung silently inward, and Kenneth, my right hand, appeared. "She has arrived."

I nodded and gestured for him to let her in.

He stepped aside, and Eve appeared. Kenneth bowed out of the room and shut the door behind her. My gaze riveted to her, something pulling at me. It made me want to stare at her for hours. She was bright and brilliant, an impossible beauty.

What the hell was I thinking?

Bright and brilliant? An impossible beauty? They were ridiculous, poetic words, and I never spoke like that. Never thought like that.

What the bloody hell was happening to me?

I reached for my flask and took a sip.

She eyed it. "Seriously, I think you have a problem."

Aye, I had a problem. I couldn't get pissed. Had other problems, too, but we wouldn't be discussing them.

She strode into the room and stopped in front of the massive fireplace, the warm glow lighting up her silver and pink hair like gems. My fingertips itched to touch the silky strands, and I clenched a fist. I was going off the rails, here.

Ever since the Dark Moon curse had taken my father, I'd avoided attachments, including sex. Abstinence was apparently coming back to bite me in the arse, because I couldn't keep my eyes off Eve. And the thoughts that went through my head...

Fates, she'd run screaming.

It'd be best for both of us if she did.

I clenched my fists, wanting—*needing*—to get back into the ring to fight. It was the only thing that could satisfy the beast inside me. Running under the moonlight was good, but fighting was better. My wolf would never attack pack, but as a human, I could trade blows without a problem.

"Did you find out who made the potion?" I asked, looking away from her.

"Yes. She's a potion master in Magic Side, Chicago. Works for Damian Malek. My friend Carrow is trying to arrange a meeting."

Magic Side. It was a massive magical metropolis, and Damian Malek was its unofficial criminal king. Fortunately, I knew the fallen angel. "Tell your friend she needn't bother. I'll get us a meeting."

"Really? You have dealings with him?"

"Not business." My pack didn't deal in anything illegal. Most of our money was made in two areas, security and whisky. In Guild City, pack members often acted as security forces for hire. We were loyal, good fighters. A natural fit. In Scotland, at our ancestral grounds and the place to which we returned in order to run beneath the full moon, we ran a successful distillery. "But I'll arrange a meeting."

"All right. Did you find the person who gave Danny the business card?" she asked. "Or get sketches done of the strangers in the bar?"

I nodded. "Aye to both. It appears that Danny was involved in a side business. Blackmail."

Her jaw dropped. "The person told you that?"

"You're surprised?"

"Yes. I don't see why they'd admit they were being blackmailed if the blackmailer was dead."

"The person is pack."

"Ah, of course. You compelled them."

"They only did what nature demands and answered their Alpha."

"Sure." There was something wary in her eyes. Normally, I'd call it prey instinct. I saw it in most people and didn't think much of it. That was part of life when faced with a predator.

Not her, though. There was nothing prey-like about her. But she was worried—it was clear as day.

"What did Danny have on you?" I asked.

"Nothing. I told you, I've never met him before."

"You were in the vicinity of a blackmailer with an envelope full of cash. There's no other reasonable explanation."

Her jaw tightened. "That's my business and has nothing to do with the murder."

She believed what she was saying, that was obvious enough. And if she'd been planning to pay him, it was highly unlikely she'd change her mind and poison him instead.

I strode toward her, inspecting her closely, looking for any little tell. It was a shame she was fae, or I could use my authority as Alpha to command her to answer. It wasn't a form of compulsion—not like the vampires had —but part of the natural law of shifters.

I decided to try, anyway, instinct compelling me. "I command that you tell me what secret Danny was hiding for you."

Her eyes flared wide, shock in their brilliant depths. "You're trying to use an Alpha's Command on me?"

"Tell me what I want to know."

Her jaw clenched, and anger flashed in her eyes. Part of me wanted to believe she was fighting the command —that I had some sway over her. Instead, she spat out, "You're a bastard, you know that?"

I shouldn't be surprised the command hadn't worked. I was losing my mind, trying it on a fae. *She* was making me lose my mind.

My life had been all cold duty until she arrived. I found it satisfying to know that I was protecting my pack. It was the safest way. The *best* way.

Then she showed up, and everything went to shite.

"I'll uncover your secrets, fae. Count on it."

She glared at me. "Did the blackmail victim have any clues?"

"No. Just gratitude for Danny's death. Danny didn't have many friends, it seems."

"What about the sketches of strangers who were in Pandemonium?"

"We haven't identified any."

"Good thing I found the potion maker, then. She can tell us who she sold the potion to."

"You'd best hope so."

"Well, I'll let you know when I speak to her."

"I'm coming with you."

Her eyes flashed, as if she wanted to argue. Instead,

she pinched her lips together.

*Good.*

"I'll get us a meeting," I said. "Until then, you'll stay here."

"No, I won't."

"Don't bother arguing." Even as I said the words, I knew that I liked it when she argued. She was all fire, and the coldness in my soul responded to it even as I knew it was a bad idea.

She pointed to the collar around her neck. "There's no reason to keep me here. You can find me anytime."

I didn't want her out of my sight until I knew what she was hiding. Instinct said it was big, and I never ignored my instinct. "You're staying here. End of discussion."

"Fine." She huffed and crossed her arms. "But I'm not staying in your quarters."

I gave her a withering look. "You're not, that's correct."

She twitched, so faintly that I might have missed it.

What was that about?

No way in hell I'd ask, though.

She turned and headed to the door. "I assume your lapdog Kenneth can tell me where my room is."

"He'll see to it."

I watched her disappear, rubbing my chest absent-mindedly.

She was going to be a problem.

## 7

*Eve*

Kenneth showed me to a small but comfortably furnished room on the other side of the tower. As soon as I shut the door behind me, I leaned against it, my knees trembling.

What the hell had just happened?

Lachlan had tried the Alpha's Command on me. Every shifter in the world had to respond to an Alpha's Command. It was built into our DNA.

I might have taken a potion to make me look fae and have a fae's powers, but I was still shifter on the inside. The potion hadn't changed what I was—it had just added to it.

He'd been testing me, but somehow, I'd passed.

How the hell had I done it?

It should have been impossible. I'd felt the pull to answer, a nearly burning desire that made my throat itch and my tongue want to move. And yet, I'd kept the words down.

It had been one of my greatest fears—that one day, I'd run into an Alpha who would ask me the wrong questions. It'd been a silly fear, considering how carefully I avoided shifters. And yet, it had come true.

I dragged an unsteady hand through my hair. If he'd suspected me of being who I really was—which he might have—he'd proven to himself that I wasn't a shifter.

Just what the hell was wrong with me if I didn't have to obey commands and I couldn't shift?

I needed some air.

Shaking still, I strode to the window. It was made of diamond-shaped panes set into iron, and I pulled open one of the sides.

My room overlooked the courtyard and the city beyond. Moonlight gleamed on the grass, and the street-lamps sparkled golden. It was a rare clear night, and the light made it easy to spot the massive figure who stepped out from a side door in the tower.

Lachlan.

He strode toward Pandemonium.

I frowned, watching him.

We'd already got all the clues we could from the place. Why was he going there?

He disappeared inside the building, giving me no hint about his purpose, and I heaved a sigh and turned back to the room.

Damn, it was quiet.

My stomach rumbled. Hunger and stress. That had to be it. I'd eaten only candy bars today, and frankly, I could use another. Ten more.

If Lachlan was gone, then maybe I could quietly hit up the kitchens. It was getting late, so they might be empty. And anyway, I wanted to do a little hunting around for info.

There was something weird about Lachlan. He was just too different from the boy I remembered. Not that I'd known him well, but the man I'd just met was all coldness and duty. Broken, somehow.

Something had happened.

I slunk from the room and down the hall, seeking out the kitchens. The memory of Danny's body in the freezer made me shudder, and I vowed to avoid any chilled foods.

Unfortunately—or maybe fortunately—the kitchen wasn't empty. An older woman had her head stuck in a small refrigerator and was fishing around. She straightened and turned as soon as I entered, and her brow furrowed. "You."

"I didn't kill Danny, I promise." I held up my hands

in a placating gesture. I should have counted on any shifters that I ran into being suspicious. Pack first, after all. "I was just in the wrong place at the wrong time, and now I'm trying to figure out who really did it."

"Trying to clear your name, more like."

"Both, actually. I don't like the idea of getting blamed for a murder. Or of a murderer walking around free."

Her face softened a bit, and she dried her hands on her apron. "Well, that I can understand."

I heaved a sigh of relief. "I don't suppose you have a spare sandwich lying around?"

As if to emphasize my request, my stomach grumbled.

Her face softened further, and I knew I had her. Not that I'd intended to manipulate her, but she was the type of maternal woman who liked feeding people, and my stomach had stepped in at just the right moment to get me a bit of sympathy.

"Coming right up, dearie." She turned back to the fridge.

"Thank you." I found a seat at one of the counter stools. The kitchen was massive and homey, with butcherblock countertops and warm red walls.

"You're in the fae guild?" she asked as she worked, cutting bread and cheese.

"No. Shadow Guild."

"One of those misfits, are you?"

I could have been offended, but I chose not to be. I

liked being in the guild for weirdos. It was the only place I fit in, and all my friends were there. "I suppose you could say that."

"What's wrong with you that you're in there?"

I frowned. "Nothing's wrong with me." That wasn't true. There was definitely something *really* weird about me. Not that I'd tell her. "It's true that we're all outcasts from our species for some reason, but there's nothing wrong with us."

"Hmm."

She didn't sound convinced, so I tried a separate tactic—the storyline I'd created for myself when I'd returned to Guild City. "I'm fae, but not from here. My own Court won't welcome me back, not after what my mother did."

"And what did she do?"

"I can't really talk about it." More like, I *never* spoke about it. Simple lies were easier to keep straight than complicated ones, so that was as far as my story went. I'd never even invented a false crime for her in my head. "Anyway, I've told you plenty about me. Now you tell me a bit about you."

She gave me a skeptical look as she walked my sandwich over to me. I took it and bit in, making a grateful noise. That got her smiling, and thankfully, talking. "Not much to tell about me. Things have been too quiet since the old Alpha passed and Garreth died."

"Died?" I felt my eyebrows shoot up my forehead. "The Alpha's brother died?"

"What do you know of him? That was almost seven years past, now."

A couple years after I'd left, then. I hadn't seen him around town, so I'd just assumed he was in Scotland at the shifters' other land. "I just remember hearing the names of the original Alpha's sons years ago, but I never knew much more." I made a vague gesture. "Life on the outside, you know?"

"Well, he died. So did the father, though we don't speak of it." She shuddered.

*Why not?* I wanted to yell. Of course, I didn't. I just plastered on a sympathetic face and went digging for gold. "That must have been so hard on you. All the mourning, and with people in poor spirits."

"Aye, it was terrible, no other ways about it." She dried her already dry hands on her apron. "And the current Alpha, fate knows he's never been the same. Eschews touch and people and closeness. Hardly a shifter at all, what with him ignoring those basic pleasures. But he's a good leader—finest we ever had, truth be told. So what's it to me if he seems a wee bit distant?"

A *bit* distant? He was as far away as Antarctica. But what was this about eschewing touch and people and closeness? "So he just keeps to himself? No girlfriend or anything?"

Her brows rose. "Fancy him, do you?"

"No! Of course not."

She scowled. "What, not good enough for you? You're just a fae."

*Just a fae.* Fates, these shifters were elitist. But I didn't need to piss her off. What I needed was more info. Anything she could give me.

"That's not what I meant," I said, backpedaling my way to a Tour de France victory. Or at least, I tried to. "Just that he wouldn't ever consider the likes of me."

She nodded approvingly, as if she liked the idea of me knowing my place.

I resisted rolling my eyes and went for more questions instead. "He really is something in the ring, though, isn't he?"

"He is indeed. Only entertainment he permits himself. Though he has to fight four at once for it to be even. And I hear they're thinking of upping the number to five."

Didn't sound like entertainment to me. More like beating his demons into submission. Which, if his brother was dead, made a lot of sense.

Garreth. Dead.

I'd never spoken to him as a kid, but I'd known they were close. And he'd been gone seven years now. Along with his dad. No wonder Lachlan had turned into a bastard.

*Had* turned into one? Hell, he'd always been one,

and he was worse now. But his life had been undeniably shitty.

"Now, don't think you're getting any more information from me, lass."

"Course not." I tried to give her a winning smile. "Any chance I could trouble you for a candy bar, though?"

**8**

---

*Eve*

The next morning, my door was locked. After my recon mission, I'd made it back to my room without running into anyone and had fallen into a fitful sleep until an ungodly early hour. But now the damned door was locked.

The cook must have ratted me out. Apparently, exploring the tower wasn't one of my prisoner's privileges.

I pounded on the door. "Let me the hell out of here!"

Maybe I shouldn't have been calling attention to myself if I was trying to lie low, but it seemed that my disguise was working, and I was pissed.

No one answered the door, so I went to the window and pushed it open.

The early morning sun was just beginning to peek over the horizon—it wasn't yet six a.m. But the day was bright and clear, and I could see a half-dozen people milling around in the courtyard below. As annoyed as I was, I kept my mouth shut instead of shouting for someone to come let me out. It was one thing to catch the attention of a single passerby in the hall—I could dose them with a potion to make them forget—but there wasn't much I could do against so many people.

I *could* fit out the window, though.

Had Lachlan not remembered I was fae? Was he testing me?

I shivered.

Maybe he didn't fully believe my disguise.

That was nothing a little wing action couldn't fix. Anyway, I didn't want to cower in my room like I was guilty.

I wasn't.

Not of *that* crime, at least.

I called upon my wings and climbed onto the windowsill, then launched myself into the air. I couldn't see the sparkle of my wings since they were behind me, but they were bright. I'd catch enough eyes to prove I was fae.

As I flew down into the courtyard, I could hear

people talking. I landed gracefully and called my wings back into my body.

*Thank you, Liora.*

I spun around, turning to face the main tower.

An angry guard came toward me, his face set in stern lines. He had the stride of a rhinoceros and the shoulders to match. I pulled a tiny vial of stunning powder from the leather bracelet at my wrist and subtly uncorked it.

He stopped right in front of me. "You're not permitted to try to escape."

I raised a brow. "Escape? Is that what you think I was doing?"

He gripped my arm.

"Not today, Satan." I stomped on his foot, then blew a blast of powder into his face.

His eyes rolled back in his head, and he collapsed liked a downed tree.

I stepped over him, muttering, "If I were trying to escape, you never would have caught me."

The eyes of the onlookers burned into me as I strode back toward the tower. They were suspicious, and I could feel it like a brand.

Maybe I needed to stop knocking the guards out. This was twice, now, that I'd assaulted them, and that surely wasn't earning me any favors. I just needed to get ahold of my temper.

The main room of the tower was empty except for

Lachlan, who strode toward me, his expression thunderous. "You aren't supposed to be out of your room."

"I don't appreciate the lock." I pointed to the golden collar around my neck. "Especially when I'm forced to wear this."

"I don't appreciate *you* sneaking around and quizzing my pack about me."

"That's hardly what I was doing." I crossed my arms. "Have you arranged a meeting with Damian?"

"I have, in fact. We will depart now."

"Now? It's midnight in Magic Side."

"Damian is a night owl. And conveniently, he'll be at a place I know."

"All right." Inconveniently, my stomach chose that moment to growl. I'd *just* eaten.

His brow lowered. "Are you hungry?"

I shrugged. "It's breakfast time, isn't it?"

"Let's get you fed." He sounded annoyed about it.

"I can wait. Let's talk to Damian." He was our one lead. I didn't want to keep him waiting.

"He'll be fine. Come on." He turned and strode toward the kitchens.

I followed, staring up at him. He looked determined to get me breakfast. It was almost...protective.

Weird.

It didn't take long for the cook to put together a bacon sandwich, and we were on our way. Fortunately, I'd already packed a bag of potions in the ether—a nifty little trick that allowed me to carry magic anywhere with me—and I'd dressed for the occasion. "How are we getting there?" I asked, following Lachlan back to the main room.

"Transport charm."

"You have one?"

"Of course I do."

*Right.* Transport charms might be rare, but he was the Alpha of a wealthy pack.

I swallowed the last bit of sandwich. "Lead the way, then."

He dug into his pocket and pulled out the charm. "Ready?"

I nodded.

He hesitated briefly, then stuck his hand out, his face in hard lines. Generally, when one traveled by transport charm, it was ideal to link hands in order to ensure that the ether took both people to the same destination. But Lachlan did *not* look like he wanted to touch me.

And oh, did it burn.

*Dog.*

The old insult flared to life in my mind, and I swallowed hard. It was the one moment of weakness I allowed myself before reaching out and gripping his hand.

The frisson of electric tension that traveled up my arm was so unexpected that I almost dropped his hand.

It was like touching a live wire—but good. Somehow, the fact that I hated him made it all the more intense.

I drew an unsteady breath and didn't make eye contact as he threw the transport charm to the ground. A cloud of silver smoke burst upward, and I followed him into it.

The ether picked us up and spun us through space, making my stomach lurch as we traveled a farther distance than I was used to. A few moments later, the ether spat us out in the middle of a mini Las Vegas. Cold Chicago wind whipped down the street, and I pushed my hair out of my eyes to get a better look.

It was seedier than the real Las Vegas, that was for sure, with an air of lawlessness about the place. The buildings, apparently converted industrial spaces, were decorated with tacky neon signs that advertised every-thing from gambling dens and strip clubs to pawn shops and fried chicken.

"Which part of Magic Side is this?" I asked. Magic Side was an all-supernatural island hidden just offshore of the Chicago lakefront. Humans had no idea it was there, but it was one of the largest all-magical cities in America.

"The Midway Dens. A lot of gambling, not a lot of rules."

"That's for sure." I watched a massive man do a strip-tease on top of a roof. He was dressed as an elephant, and the trunk was his... My brows rose to my hairline.

"Quick, hand me some pearls so I can clutch them." Lachlan gave me a confused look, and I just shook my head. "Don't worry about it. Apparently, you don't get out much. Which way to Damian Malek?"

"This way." He led me down the crowded street.

I stuck close. People parted like the Red Sea as we passed, no doubt because Lachlan scared the shit out of them. The neon glow of the signs only emphasized his hard ruthlessness. Music blared from the bars we passed, and the scent of booze filled the air.

The street seemed unusually clear for such a popular time of night, and the reason became obvious when two cars buzzed down the street, their engines roaring to the cheer of the crowds.

Drag racing.

"We're here." Lachlan stopped in front of a heavy wooden door and nodded at the hulking bouncer, who pulled it open to admit us.

Lachlan stuck close to me as we entered, though he made a point not to touch me. It was almost as if he thought he were allergic to me but wanted to protect me all the same.

As soon as we made it inside the crush of people, I realized why Lachlan knew this place.

There was a massive fight ring in the middle of the cavernous room. Bare lightbulbs hung from the ceiling, illuminating the people who crowded around the ring. It was a bare bones place, though the clientele was anything but. People were dressed to the nines, flashing designer labels everywhere, though some wore more understated attire that screamed "real money."

"You're really into this fighting thing, aren't you?" I asked.

"Everyone needs a hobby."

It was his only hobby, it seemed. "And Damian?"

"He needs a hobby, too."

Was he also beating his own demons to death?

I didn't ask. There was no point in getting to know either man. It was a terrible idea, in fact.

Once again, the crowd parted as we made our way deeper into the room. There weren't many shifters here that I could see, but it didn't matter. Supernaturals could sense the strength of each other's power, and Lachlan had enough to make anyone want to get out of the way. Combined with his stature and the look in his eyes, no one wanted to land on his bad side.

He led me straight to the bar and found a free space in the middle. I sidled up to a man leaning over his whisky glass. He turned to me, his eyes brightening as he leered. "Hey, Tinker Bell."

I heard a faint growl from behind me but didn't need to look back to know it was Lachlan.

The man turned green and stumbled off his stool, backing away without taking his drink.

I turned to Lachlan. "Really, Cujo?"

He frowned at me, and I almost thought I saw

surprise in his eyes.

Not at the joke, that was for sure. Lachlan wasn't big into laughing.

No, he seemed confused that he'd growled.

***

*Lachlan*

What the hell was I doing? Trying to mark my territory?

It was common with mates, but she wasn't my mate. *That* woman was long gone. Dead, for all I knew. So what was it about this fae?

I looked down at her, taking in the surprise in her eyes. I felt it, too, and despised it.

There had been plenty I hadn't liked about my life—the loss of my brother, the fact that I'd had to put down my crazed father, the looming threat of the Dark Moon curse. But one thing that had always been rock steady for me was the fact that I knew who I was and what I needed to do: lead my pack. It had informed all my decisions and given me a reliable bedrock when making decisions.

This small fae was throwing me for a loop.

I turned back to the barman, who'd stopped in front

of us. He had a sharp look to his eyes, and it was clear that he was no ordinary bartender. No, he was part of Damian's network—a series of spies and minions who kept tabs on Magic Side for him.

"We're here to see Damian Malek," I said.

He nodded. "A moment."

I directed my voice to Eve but didn't look directly at her. "A drink?"

"Yes. But not a strong one." She glanced around, wary.

It was smart not to want to lose focus in a place like this. It was built for fun and games, but it wore a slick veneer of danger that should be respected.

Another bartender stopped by, and I ordered two beers, passing her one. I ignored mine, preferring the burn of my own whisky.

The original bartender returned a moment later. "He will see you now."

We followed him through the bar to a raised booth in the corner. Damian was the sort of man to sit with his back to two walls, ever alert. There was much in his past I didn't know—almost everything, in fact—but I also didn't care to ask. We shared a fondness for the ring, and that was enough.

Damian rose as we stepped up to the table. Tall and broad shouldered, with a ruthlessness to his eyes, he was the kind of man I recognized. Had he been a shifter, he would have been an Alpha. As it was, he sat at the top of the criminal pecking order in Magic Side, a fallen angel with more stains on his soul and more connections than anyone else I knew.

"Lachlan. And friend. Please sit." Damian's eyes traveled over Eve, and though there was nothing lascivious in their depths, I still felt myself taking a step closer to her.

I couldn't control this damned protectiveness, no matter what I did. It made no sense.

Damian's brows quirked, interest lighting in his eyes. I ignored him and sat at the table. Eve took the chair next to me. I didn't introduce her, not wanting him to know her name.

I was losing my bloody mind.

"To what do I owe the pleasure?" Damian asked.

"We are here to ask a favor." I didn't like asking it. Didn't like owing anyone. But my packmate—no matter how much of a weasel he'd been—deserved to have his murderer brought to justice, and Damian could help make that happen.

"So you know the way of things in Magic Side." He smiled, but it didn't reach his eyes.

Magic Side, especially this lawless part, was run on favors. Damian owned a massive tower in the respectable part of town and did most of his business from there, but he had plenty of dealings in the darker part of the city, and that's what we needed now.

"We need to find someone," I said.

"I'm sure we can come to an arrangement. Who is it?"

"We need an audience with a woman named the Apothecary. Alia."

Damian's brows rose once more. "I'm afraid I can't get you an audience with her—she determines that for herself. But I can tell you how to find her."

"And in return?" I asked.

"A fight."

I felt Eve stiffen next to me, her confusion palpable.

I wasn't surprised. Damian liked a good bout in the ring. And like me, he had a hard time finding a proper opponent. We'd gone up against each other several times, and our record was even.

"Do I need to win?" I could, given the proper incentive. Though our record was fifty-fifty, this was proper motivation to ensure a win.

"No." Damian smiled. "I'm not bothered by who wins. We'll both end up beat to a pulp, either way."

"What the hell are you talking about?" Eve demanded.

I nodded toward the ring behind me. A roar from the crowd happened to go up at the same time. "A bit of that. For fun."

She looked back and forth between us, horrified. "How is that fun for you?"

I rubbed at the back of my neck and shrugged. "Just is."

# 9

*Eve*

I stared at the two men, aghast. They were insane.

Officially *insane.*

But if this was what it took to clear my name, then by all means, they should be allowed to beat the shit out of each other. Weirdos.

Damian smiled and stood. "Shall we?"

Lachlan rose, and I followed suit. "Where to?" he asked.

"That basement, I think." Damian skirted around the table and led the way through the crowded bar.

Was the basement an extra-exclusive club? Members only?

The crowd parted to let us pass, and we reached a

dark door in the corner. It was unguarded but locked. Within seconds, the same bartender who had arranged for our meeting appeared. He unlocked the door, and we climbed down the metal stairs. Bare lightbulbs illuminated the way, and when we reached the bottom, Damian flicked on several lights.

Yeah, this definitely wasn't an exclusive, members-only club.

It was just a basement. There was a ratty old ring in the corner, some of the side ropes stripped of the padding that normally protected them.

"You two are serious about this?" I couldn't help but ask.

Neither answered, so I found a rusty folding chair to sit in. The two men strode toward the ring, taking their shirts off as they walked. Both were magnificently formed, and I hated the way my eyes strayed toward Lachlan. Damian was gorgeous, no question about it, but I couldn't look away from the raw intensity in Lachlan's eyes. It took my breath.

I could see the wolf inside him, desperate to come out. His eyes flared a more brilliant green, and he clenched his fists.

Damian grinned, then climbed into the ring.

Lachlan followed.

There was no one to call the start of the match, but they didn't need it. Damian struck first, so fast and hard that I was shocked Lachlan managed to dodge.

He did, however, and landed a glancing blow to Damian's side. The fallen angel was quick and managed to avoid most of the hit, returning one of his own.

Immediately, I understood why Damian had wanted the fight. Lachlan was surely one of the few who could give him a fair match. The memory of Lachlan fighting four men back at Pandemonium came to mind.

Who the hell was going to win this one?

The hits came harder and faster as the match progressed. I flinched each time one of them made contact with the other's face, but neither ever seemed like they wanted to quit. Rather, it seemed like they *enjoyed* it. Not just landing the hits, but taking them.

I knew what demons Lachlan was trying to exorcise—his dead brother, at the very least—but what about Damian?

As the fight progressed, it didn't take long for me to start rooting for Lachlan. I couldn't help it. He was a bastard, a cruel one who'd made my life miserable, but as he took hit after hit—and delivered just as many of his own—I felt my fists clenching and my heart racing.

*Come on, just knock him out.*

I wanted this to be over with, for fates' sake. Blood was dripping from a cut on the right side of Lachlan's brow, and his sides would be brilliant with bruises in a few hours. Damian didn't look any better. The fallen angel would have at least one black eye tomorrow—maybe two.

But they just kept going.

It got to the point where I hated seeing Lachlan take a hit. Something clenched inside me every time Damian landed a punch.

Eventually, they began to slow. Lachlan favored his right side, and it seemed like something might be wrong with Damian's hand.

Finally, I couldn't take it anymore and surged to my feet. "Enough!"

They ignored me, continuing to hurl blows at each other. It was almost as if they'd entered some kind of meditative trance, and maybe they had. Hell, this hadn't been a hardship at all for Lachlan. He was *enjoying* it.

I wasn't, though. There was too much blood from split lips and split brows. Too many bruises waiting to form. If Lachlan was laid out for too long, we wouldn't be able to find the Apothecary.

Enough was enough.

I climbed into the ring, wriggling between the ropes, and got right up next to them to shout, "Stop!"

They both jerked, then turned to me, blinking. Surprised to see me.

"Get out," Lachlan growled, his eyes brilliant green with his wolf.

"No. You're going to stop now. You need to be fit enough to help me find Alia, and this isn't going to help."

He drew in a shuddering breath and stepped back,

eying Damian. He jerked his head to the side, indicating that Damian should step away from me. "Get out of the ring, Eve. We'll stop, but it's dangerous to charge in here."

"Yeah, yeah." But I could see the worry in his eyes.

It's not like they were going to snap now that I'd pulled them out of their trance, but he had a point. One of them could have thrown the other onto me, and that would have sucked.

Quickly, I climbed out of the ring.

A few moments later, the two men followed. Both looked like hell, but I ignored it. I also ignored the fact that I was worried about Lachlan. It was stupid.

I glanced at Damian. "Well, where is the Apothecary?"

He looked from Lachlan to me, finally seeming to settle on the idea that it was over. With a sigh, he grabbed his discarded T-shirt from the ground and mopped the blood off his face. He looked more like a fallen angel than ever, with his swollen lips and dark eyes. "You can find her here, in the Midway Dens. At the top of the old bottling building. But I suggest you wait until early morning. Her guards should be less alert then. It's the quiet hour."

"Guards?" I asked, watching Lachlan out of the corner of my eye. He'd bent to pick up his shirt, and he was moving gingerly.

"She takes security seriously," Damian said. He

looked at Lachlan, sizing him up. "You only want answers, correct? You won't hurt her?"

Lachlan nodded. "I give you my word."

"I could try to call her and tell her you're coming, but I don't want her knowing it was me who sent you. So keep that to yourself."

"Will do," Lachlan said.

"Good. And one last thing—I'd suggest approaching from the alley. You can expect three, maybe four, demons."

"Thank you." Lachlan pulled his shirt on over his head and looked at me. "Ready?"

I nodded my thanks to Damian, then followed Lachlan from the basement, up the stairs, through the heaving crowd, and out into the cold night air.

"Where to until morning?" I asked, eying his injuries worriedly. "You need to get cleaned up. Maybe take a healing potion. I have one."

"No potions," he growled.

"Sure, whatever, Cujo."

"Cujo?"

"You know, the killer dog from Steven King."

The edge of his lips quirked up in a reluctant smile, and he winced. "We'll find a hotel to spend the next few hours. I heal fast, so I should be mostly good by dawn."

"Suit yourself." Why he was so against potions, I had no idea.

We found a seedy motel a few streets down. There

wasn't much else in this part of town, and it would do for our purposes. Lachlan looked too rough to be let into any of the nicer places, anyway.

The motel was one of those two-story establishments with doors that exited onto the outdoor walkway. Very 1960s America. Lachlan insisted that we share a room. A plaque on the wall advertised that Elvis had once stayed in the very same suite.

"Last time it was updated, too, I bet," I muttered.

Fortunately, there were two beds. I flopped onto one while Lachlan headed toward the bathroom. "I'll be in the shower."

I heard the water go on, creaking as the pipes filled. A few minutes later, I heard a pained groan and had to assume he'd climbed in.

I thunked my head back against the old headboard. What the hell was I doing, thinking about him in the shower? That was all kinds of bad news.

I should be knackered, but I wasn't. Even though it was after three a.m. here, I was still on London time.

A few moments later, Lachlan emerged from the bathroom. He had a towel wrapped around his waist, revealing a broad expanse of damp, bare chest. My heartrate picked up, and I swallowed hard, looking away. "You didn't want to put on trousers, at least?"

"Too stiff."

"I should have my own room."

"I'm not letting you out of my sight in this town, collar or no collar."

He had a point. In Guild City, there were people with the skill to remove the collar, but no one would dare, since *he'd* put it on me. That wouldn't be the case in Magic Side.

He turned to the sink. Out of the corner of my eye, I saw him flinch.

Concern pierced me, and I slid off of the bed. "Are you *sure* you don't want a healing potion?"

"I'm sure." His voice was rough. "I'll heal quickly."

"Well, you're still bleeding from that cut on your brow." I went to the bathroom and knelt down to fish around in the cupboard for a first aid kit, hoping we'd get lucky.

Lachlan made a low noise in his throat, and I looked up, realizing that he stood right over me. He hadn't moved, either. I'd been the one to kneel here—which now seemed like an insane idea. He looked like a mountain towering above.

Tension tightened the air between us, making every inch of my skin prickle as heat flushed through me. Fortunately, I spotted an old first aid kit and grabbed it, then hopped to my feet. I waved it in the air like a ninny and said, "Found it."

He frowned. "A plaster?"

"And antiseptic. With any luck, there will be paracetamol in here as well."

His gaze lingered too long on me, so I popped open the plastic container and fished out the alcohol wipe and wrapped plaster. Before I could stop myself—or before he could stop me—I tore open the wipe and smoothed it over his cut brow.

Up close, he was even more beautiful. Terrifying, too, with the way his eyes flared bright green.

His wolf.

I swallowed hard, my skin igniting as heat flushed through me.

He was so much bigger than me. So much stronger. But somehow, I knew he'd never hurt me. Not physically, at least. He'd hurt me plenty when we were children, and he'd have no problem locking me up if he thought I was the killer. But right now, with the way he looked down at me...

"What is it about you?" he murmured. He lifted a hand, holding it near my temple. Close, but no contact. His full lips parted, and his eyes flashed with desire.

*He wants me.*

I knew it like I knew my own name. It was written all over his face. It made my breath catch in my throat and my mind go blank.

It was crazy, but I wanted to sway forward. To close the distance between us.

"I don't know what you mean." Shivers raced over my skin. All of my previous hatred, my anger...it was hard to recall them right now, when we stood so close. It was insane. But something drew me to him, pulling at my soul.

The mate bond?

No. I didn't feel it. I couldn't, not as long as I wore the necklace that made me fae.

Yet still, I wanted him. I was a terrible, shallow person to want the man who'd been so cruel to me.

"There's something about you." He leaned close and inhaled, sniffing me.

I stiffened. A wolf's ability to smell was one of their primary gifts. Could he recognize me this way?

*No.*

Changing my species with potions had changed that as well. I'd covered all my bases.

He withdrew his head and met my gaze, his eyes dark, the pupils dilated. His gaze moved to my pointed fae ears, then back to my eyes. "I feel like you're someone you're not. And what I'm thinking isn't even possible."

A chill chased away the heat that had surged through me. "You've had a real knock to the head." I stepped back. "A little rest will put you to rights."

He stared after me, his brow creased, and I walked to the far bed, then curled up and faced away from him. "I'm going to sleep."

He made a noncommittal noise, and I heard him climb onto the bed next to mine. As I stared blindly at the wall, I couldn't help but be aware of every one of his movements. Of his gaze, burning into my back.

I still wanted him.

I'd walked away from him, but damn it, my entire body still buzzed. It was crazy.

He was growing more suspicious, there was no question. My disguise was good—only a few people in the world even knew that it was possible to do what I'd done—but every minute in his company was a step closer to him learning the truth.

## 10

*Eve*

Just before dawn, we departed our seedy motel and headed for the old bottling plant. It was located at the edge of the Midway Dens, and we had to cross through the part of town that had been so busy last night.

In the early light, the streets were empty of drag racers, and everything was silent, save for a few pigeons that strutted from bin to bin, gorging themselves on discarded takeaways from the night before.

Lachlan and I hadn't spoken much, but I could feel his gaze constantly on me. It was almost as if the further we got from his suspicion that I was the murderer, the more he suspected me of other things.

I shivered, careful not to look his way.

Finally, I caught sight of the tall old factory building where Alia lived. The bricks on one side were painted white beneath a black script reading *The Bottling Plant*.

Creative name, that.

"Let's head for the alley," Lachlan said.

I nodded and followed him through the cold, dark streets to the narrow alley at the back. The brick buildings rose tall on either side of us, looming toward the pinkening sky. Fire escapes climbed the walls, rickety metal stairs leading to wooden doors. They covered the back of the building, zigzagging in rows down the side, which gave the wall the appearance of an old-school video game. The demon guards could be behind any of the doors, watching from the windows for intruders to approach.

"Demons," he murmured. "Can you smell them?"

I shook my head. I'd never had proper shifter senses, and I certainly didn't have them now that I'd spent so long relying on the fae magic I'd bought myself with potions.

"Four. Maybe five," he said.

Damn. Damian had said only three or four.

He looked down at me. "Use those wings of yours to get out of the way."

I bristled. "I can fight."

"Do so from the sky. Out of range."

Worry glinted in his eyes, and I frowned at him. "I

didn't expect you to be so concerned. You think I might be the murderer."

"Just get out of the way."

I scowled but nodded. I fought best from the air, anyway, where I had a good vantage point for hurling my potion bombs. I called upon my magic and felt my wings flare to life behind me.

Lachlan watched them, his gaze unreadable.

I took off into the air, hovering high above the alley.

A low shout sounded from the building where the demon guards were hiding. They knew we were here.

My heart jumped into my throat. I called on the bag that I stored in the ether, then plunged my hand in and grabbed a potion bomb.

In the alley below, Lachlan stepped away from the wall and approached the fire escape stairs. Why hadn't he shifted yet? Surely he was safer in wolf form.

A demon stepped out onto one of the balconies about four stories up. With his pale gray skin, he would have looked almost human if not for the sawed-off horns and black claws. He raised a crossbow and aimed it at Lachlan.

Was the bolt silver tipped?

Fear rocketed through me.

Before he could fire, I chucked a potion bomb at him. The glass globe hurtled through the air, smashing against his chest and spraying him with brilliant red potion. He shrieked as the acid ate into him, dropping his crossbow and stumbling backward toward the brick wall.

While I'd been attacking him, four more demons had come out onto other fire escapes. Lachlan moved insanely fast, racing up the stairs and grabbing one of the attackers by the collar, then heaving him over the side. The demon screamed as he fell and crashed to the ground in a heap.

Now that Lachlan was on the fire escape, the other three demons couldn't get a clear shot at him from their positions on the other staircases. They'd have to fire their crossbows between the metal slats of the stairs, and it would never work.

They had a great shot at *me*, though.

One of them turned his bow up toward me, and my skin iced. As he fired, I flew upward as fast as I could, narrowly avoiding the bolt. He swore and reloaded, and I dove back down, gripping a potion bomb tight. When I was close enough, I hurled my potion bomb at his head. The bottle flew through the air, smashing against his skull and coating him in a pale blue liquid that froze him solid. He toppled forward.

On the fire escape below him, Lachlan charged at the other two demons who were scrambling down the fire escapes in search of a clean shot. As he sprinted toward them, deep green magic swirled around him, and he shifted midstride. One moment, he was a man;

the next, he was a massive black wolf, bigger than any I'd ever seen.

He was magnificent.

He reached the demons a half second later and tore out the nearer demon's throat. The other demon tried to get a shot off, but Lachlan was too fast. He spat out the dead demon and lunged at the second, and blood sprayed as he went for the throat a second time.

I looked away, searching for more attackers, but there were none, thank fates.

The demons who'd fallen into the alley below were already starting to disappear. Unlike humans or other supernaturals, demons couldn't really be killed. Technically, they weren't even supposed to be out of the Underworld, though there were many ways around that rule. Once they were killed on earth, their bodies disappeared, and they woke up in whatever Underworld they'd come from.

It made cleanup easy, at least.

I flew down to Lachlan, who shifted back into his human form in the blink of an eye, the process hidden by a swirl of magic that matched his eyes. The older and more powerful you were, the easier it was to change forms. For Lachlan, it was as easy as breathing.

I landed next to him, and he turned to me, his chest heaving and his eyes still bright green with his wolf. His gaze flashed between my wings and my face, something unrecognizable in his expression. It was almost confusion, or perhaps recognition. Desire, definitely, like the heat of battle had warmed his blood as well as his fighting instinct. He stepped toward me. Heat flared in his eyes, and he looked straight at my mouth.

I gasped as I stared back at him, every inch of me prickling with awareness. His gaze never left my lips.

Was he going to try to kiss me?

Would I let him?

He stepped back abruptly, and I blinked. What the hell had that been?

"You did well," he said. "We should head to the top."

I nodded. "Of course. There could be more guards."

He turned and climbed the fire escape to the next interior door, ignoring the disintegrating bodies of the demons. I followed him, my mind racing. I had no idea what had just happened, but it had been *a moment* of some kind.

Just what *kind* of moment, I couldn't say.

We were halfway up the building when we reached the next level on the fire escape. The door was locked, but Lachlan gave it a swift kick, and we were in.

He held out a hand, indicating that I should wait while he checked the room.

His protectiveness was...weird.

I'd never had someone like that in my life. True, my friends wanted to protect me, but this had a different flavor to it. We protected each other. *This* felt decidedly one-sided. I gave him a second to check out the space first, then followed. I couldn't stand around forever like a damsel in distress.

The hallway inside was dark and quiet, old and industrial. The entire floor felt empty, and smelled it, too, dusty and disused.

"I think only the top floor is occupied," Lachlan whispered.

No doubt he was using his lupine hearing and super sense of smell.

Together, we quietly crept up the stairs, flight after flight. It was an easy journey, with no demons jumping out of the darkened corners.

Too easy.

The hair on the back of my neck stood up, every instinct going on red alert as we reached the landing on the top floor. A dark door stood at the end, closed tightly.

The apothecary was on the other side, but there were no demon guards.

Ahead of me, Lachlan stepped forward, then stopped abruptly. I slammed into his back, letting out a whoosh of air. "What happened?" I asked.

"I'm stuck."

"Stuck?" I frowned. "What do you mean?" I looked down at his feet.

He tried to lift them but couldn't.

*Shit.*

I tried my own feet. Also stuck. A faint mist began to

drift down from the ceiling, acrid and dark. I coughed, my lungs burning.

"A trap," he said.

Heart pounding, I crouched down to get out of the cloud of smoke and inspect the slick liquid that glued our feet to the floor. It coated the entire walkway, so taking off our shoes wouldn't do it.

In front of me, Lachlan crouched low as well. We were too close, bumping into each other, but we managed to stay out of the worst of the smoke.

"Do you know what it is?" he asked.

"Maybe." I knelt as low as I could and sniffed the shiny liquid on the floor. Almonds and evergreen—stomach-turningly strange, but also the signature scent of Kerinius sap, a rare ingredient that could be tempered to become the stickiest substance on earth.

Hope flared, and I dug around in the potion bag that I hadn't yet returned to the ether. "I think I can neutralize it."

"What about the smoke?" He coughed quietly, clearly trying to hide the fact that we were out there.

"Hold your breath," I said, "because there's nothing I can do about that."

Finally, my hand closed over a narrow cylinder of truth potion. The potion was rare and expensive, and a weird choice for a magically sticky floor, but its main ingredient, Arcanium Root, was going to come in very handy in combatting the Kerinius sap. Quickly, I sprinkled the potion around our feet. It made the sap glow briefly, then melt away into a sloshy liquid, which spread quickly and neutralized the entire floor.

Lungs burning from holding my breath, I grabbed Lachlan's hand and dragged him forward. The floor was still a little sticky, but not unbearably so.

As we reached the door, it swung open, revealing a pretty, dark-haired woman with a star tattooed by her eye. She wore a silk floral bathrobe and had her dark hair piled on top of her head. Seeing us, she leaned against the door frame. "Well, well, well. You've impressed me. Eve?"

I nodded and gasped, "Please let us in. We have only questions."

She frowned, looking between the two of us. "You killed my demons."

"I'll pay for replacements," Lachlan said. It was a good offer. It was expensive to pay sorcerers to get them out of the Underworld. "Or I can ask around if any shifter security forces want to relocate to Magic Side."

That was an even better offer. Shifters were the most coveted security forces out there, far better than demons. Way more loyal.

She raised her brows, clearly recognizing the value of the offer. "Well, then. Come on in."

She waved us forward, and we hurried inside. I gasped, trying to catch my breath, as she strolled around to stand in front of us and eyed me up and down.

"Was it the smell that allowed you to identify the sap?" she asked.

I nodded.

"Impressive." She turned and walked into the high-ceilinged loft. It was a massive space, decorated with modern furniture and thousands of books and plants. Faerie lights glittered among the rafters, and I wondered how she'd got hold of them. Huge glass windows provided a view of Chicago, and it had to be spectacular at night.

She turned back to us, her robe swishing. "What do you need? Surely not a potion, considering your skills, Eve."

"You know me?" I asked.

"Fae, with crazy-colored hair and an unusual skill for potions? I guessed. Also, I know your friend Seraphia."

"Nice to meet you—"

Lachlan cut right to the point. "We're here about a potion you sold. An Ageratina potion."

Her gaze turned dark, and she looked away, her face twisting slightly. "That one. Yes."

"It's a killing potion," I said. "You knew that when you sold it."

"*Sold* isn't quite the word I would use." She looked back, anger flashing in her eyes. "Did you not wonder why there were so many guards?"

"That's not normal?"

"That many? No. Usually, I have a couple. But ever since that miserable shifter came to my door and threatened me, I've been wary."

"A shifter?" Lachlan asked.

"Yes. And he didn't pay fair price."

I frowned at her, thinking how horrible it would be to have someone compel me to make something so dangerous. "What happened?"

"Nothing terribly surprising. He broke in and forced me to make the potion. I didn't see much of him, given the hood."

"What *did* you see?" Lachlan asked.

She watched him for a long second, chewing on her lip. "I want something in return."

"We're trying to catch a murderer," I said. "Surely you can help us."

She flinched slightly. "Who was murdered?"

"He was a right bastard," Lachlan said. "But he was part of my pack."

She heaved a sigh. "I'm not helping you without payment, though. Rent isn't cheap here, nor are my supplies."

I looked toward the corner, where she had several tables piled high with tiny bottles of ingredients and bundles of dried herbs. "What do you want?"

She looked right at me. "The recipe to your most valuable potion."

I frowned at her. "Which one is that?"

"You tell me. But it had better be good. *Real* good."

Shit. Shit. Shit.

I knew which one my most valuable potion was. Could I fake it and give her another?

"I'll make you take a truth serum," she said, "so I know it's the best one."

"You're ruthless," I replied, though I respected her for it.

She shrugged. "What can I say? Bitches get shit done."

Truer words.

I looked between her and Lachlan, debating, but the contest didn't take long. We needed this. I hiked a thumb at Lachlan. "Go out on the balcony. You can't hear this."

"Of course I can."

"These are proprietary recipes," I said. "I've never told another living soul this one, and I'm not telling you, too."

He frowned, then nodded and strode toward the huge glass windows that led to the front balcony. Once he was safely outside, I turned to Alia. "Can you set up a sound barrier? And you're going to need to make a blood oath not to share this with anyone."

She nodded, then went to her table and picked up a bundle of herbs that had been tied together with various colors of ribbon. I recognized the little bundle—

I'd made several myself. It would make it so no one could hear what we said.

She picked up a lighter, a few vials of potion, and a pen and paper, then went to a tiny sitting area and gestured for me to follow. My heart thundered as she set us up around the little table, laying out a contract for a blood oath—no surprise a woman like her kept them on hand—and the vial of truth potion.

She lit the bundle of herbs on fire and made a circle around us. I felt it when the magic fell into place. Lachlan wouldn't hear.

"This had better be good," she said, pricking her thumb with a blade and letting a brilliant red drop of blood fall onto the contract.

"It is."

She handed the contract to me, and I scanned it, seeing that she would die a slow, agonizing death if she told my secret to anyone. "Glad to see you don't pull your punches."

She smiled. "I know what a good spell is worth."

"Then hold on to your hat." I picked up the truth potion and sniffed it, then knocked it back.

As I felt it fizz through my veins, I looked at Alia. We'd have been friends if we lived in the same place, I was sure of it. We had similar survival instincts. A willingness to do whatever it took. I could sense it in her.

"Well?" she said.

"I'm not fae." I called upon my wings, letting them

flare behind me. Then I put my hand on the table and made grass grow straight out of the wood.

"Holy fates." Her eyes widened. "You're not fae, yet you can do *that*?"

"Yep. Lightning, too, and these wings aren't just for show. All fae magics." I tapped my pointed ears. "Not just a glamour."

Her breathing grew short, excitement glinting in her eyes. "You changed your species using potions. It should be impossible."

"It's not." I gave a wry laugh. "Not easy, but it's possible."

She shook her head. "You have to tell me."

"That's why we're sitting here." I held up my necklace so she could see it. "I've enchanted this with a potion. It's too volatile to drink, but if you wear an object that is regularly anointed with it...voila, you become fae." I reached for the pen and paper, then began to write out the recipe.

"What are you really, then? If you're not fae?"

"That's not part of the deal." I handed her the finished recipe. "That will only tell you how to change your species to fae. But if you work on it, you might be able to manage another species. Burn that paper after you've memorized it."

She scanned the ingredient list, her brows rising. "These are rare. Expensive."

"Which is why I'm always broke." Well, that and damned Danny. Poor bastard.

She shook her head, impressed. "Amazing. Truly amazing." Her gaze flicked to the window, where Lachlan stood with his back to us. "He believes you're fae, I assume."

"He'd better."

**11**

---

*Eve*

After I answered some of Alia's recipe-related questions, we let Lachlan back into the flat.

His gaze moved between us. "All good?"

"All good." Alia nodded once. "So, you want to know what he looked like?"

"We want to know everything you know," Lachlan said.

"All right. Like I said, I couldn't see much. But I did see his eyes. Pure black."

Lachlan stiffened. "Pure black eyes?"

"No whites at all." She shivered. "He was creepy. *Beyond* creepy, even though I couldn't see his face. Definitely a predator. The way he looked at me..." The shiver turned into a shudder, and I felt for her. Potion makers didn't normally end up face to face with danger unless we ran right at it.

"I'm sorry that happened to you," I said.

She gave a wry laugh. "It's far from the worst thing I've faced. Anyway, the guy." She looked Lachlan up and down. "He was about your size. Similar shape, too. Fit."

That narrowed it down a little, but not a lot. Lachlan was unusually tall and fit as hell, but he was hardly the only one.

"He didn't speak much," she said. "And when he did, his voice was rough. Like he didn't use it much. There was an intensity about him that was almost...manic. Maybe insane. I don't know, I'm no psych."

"Anything else?" I asked, wishing she knew more. It really wasn't a lot, given that I'd just shared one of the most powerful potions in existence with her.

"Yeah. Hang on." She went to her workshop table and found a box that was hidden beneath piles of potion bottles and tiny little envelopes. She pulled it out and opened it, withdrawing something small. When she returned to us, she held an object out flat in her palm. "I stole this from him."

My gaze was riveted to the massive claw in her hand. It was pitch black and looked like it could tear out my throat if she held it just right. I glanced up at Lachlan.

He looked like he'd seen a ghost.

"You stole that from him?" His voice was rough.

"He was shaky, like he was coming off a bender of some kind. When he reached into his pocket for something, this fell out." She shrugged. "A crazy guy like him, carrying this around...it had to be special to him. And I was pissed as hell at what he was making me do, so I kicked it under the table before he noticed it. Thought maybe I could use it to track him and get my potion back, but..." She shuddered.

"He scared the crap out of you, and you didn't want anything to do with him," I said.

"Basically." She looked sad. "I'm not proud of it. But you have to understand, I've just escaped hell. Literally. Hell. I want a normal life, that's all."

I could understand that.

She shoved the claw out toward Lachlan. "Anyway, take it. Maybe it will help you."

Lachlan did so, swallowing hard, his gaze fixed on the claw.

"Is it a wolf claw?" I asked.

He nodded, but there was something in his eyes that I didn't recognize. Lachlan definitely knew more than I did.

"Thank you," he said. "If that's all, we'll be going."

She nodded.

Before we left, Lachlan made a call to replace her guards. When he'd finished, we said our goodbyes quickly, and I told her that she should visit me in Guild City sometime, that maybe she'd prefer living there. She just nodded, and we left, using one of Lachlan's transportation charms to take us back.

It was early afternoon when we arrived in the middle of the courtyard that faced the Shifters' Guild tower.

I turned to Lachlan. His gaze was darker than it had ever been, the deep green turned almost black.

*All black eyes.*

Something that Alia had said had made Lachlan twitchy. Even now, he looked like his mind was a million miles away.

"You know something," I said.

Surprised, he looked down at me, his gaze clearing briefly. It was almost like he'd forgotten I was there. "I need to go see someone. You may return to your home for a short while. We can reconvene here later tonight."

"Don't keep me out of the loop now."

"I'll see you in a bit." He turned and strode off.

I stared after him, surprised. Did this mean I was off the hook?

I touched the collar at my neck.

*Nope.*

But what the hell was up with him and that claw? I wanted to chase after him to find out, but he'd made it clear he wouldn't answer my prying. Anyway, I needed a shower.

I was halfway to my place when I passed by a narrow alley leading to the back of a coffee shop. Someone shoved me from behind, forcing me into the darkened alley. I slammed against the wall, knocking the air from my lungs.

Panicked, I fought to spin around, but the person grabbed my arm and tried to drag me into the alley. The figure was huge, towering over me in a black hoodie.

Ice surged through my veins.

I kicked, nailing him in the stomach. He grunted but gripped me harder and pulled.

I screamed as I scrambled to free a potion vial from my cuff. I grabbed the first one I touched. Brilliant green flashed—acid powder, basically magical mace.

My assailant lashed out to knock me in the head, and I ducked. His blow cuffed me over the top of my skull, and pain flared.

I flipped off the top of the vial and blew the powder in his face, which was concealed by the deep shadows beneath his hood. I could only see the dark flash of his eyes, which gleamed with an unholy brilliance.

He roared in pain, releasing me and lunging backward.

I called upon my wings and launched myself into the air, desperate to get away from him.

He sprinted down the alley, one hand held over his face as he dug into his pocket. My heart raced. Did I follow him or get the hell out of there?

*Follow him.*

It didn't matter, though. He hurled something to the

ground. A silvery cloud burst forth, and he lunged inside.

A transport charm. He was gone.

Panting, mind spinning, I flew home. The entire way, I made sure to head down the middle of the busiest street in town. I was pretty sure I'd driven my attacker off, but it would be temporary.

By the time I reached the Shadow Guild tower, my heart rate had calmed, and the pain in my head had faded. I could feel the scrape on my cheek where I'd slammed into the wall, but it didn't hurt terribly.

What the hell had just happened? Had that been the killer?

*Yes.*

But why had he come after me?

I let myself into the tower, breathing a sigh of relief. No one could enter except Shadow Guild members. I'd be safe here.

"Anyone home?" I called.

Silence.

It was fine. *I'm still safe.* I climbed the stairs toward my loft, but as soon as I stepped through the door, I heard the sound of rustling from the bedroom. I stiffened, ice cascading over my skin. Who the hell was there?

*Not him.*

The tower was guarded against intruders. He couldn't get in.

Still, fear washed over me.

I picked up a potion bomb that I'd left sitting on the end table—a stunner—and crept through the small living room toward the bedroom. As I rounded the corner, a furry head popped out of one of my dresser drawers, a Mars bar clutched in its jaws.

The raccoon's eyes widened behind his black mask, and he dropped the candy bar. *Meow?*

I heard his voice in my head, and my jaw dropped at his audacity. "*Meow?* Meow, my arse. You are *not* a cat."

*Meow.*

The little bastard had said it again! The raccoon scampered out of the drawer and leapt across the bed to dive out the open window. I raced over and spotted him shimmying down the tree, fat bum and fluffy tail waving.

"Don't even think you can come back here and steal more of my candy bars!" I shouted.

The raccoon ignored me, and I flopped onto my bed. The little bastard had seriously just pretended to be a cat.

Attacked by a killer, and now dealing with a damned raccoon who somehow managed to get past the magical barriers in our tower. How was this my life?

I rubbed my hands over my eyes and got up. My stomach growled, so I went to the drawer, grabbing the Mars bar and inspecting the wrapper for damage. It looked fine, so I tore into it and shoved half in my mouth, feeling part of my stress start to immediately evaporate.

Lately, I'd taken to hiding candy everywhere. I'd always been a sweets hoarder, but that damned raccoon had turned me into a freaking squirrel. As a result, I'd lost track of half the candy bars I'd ever hidden—including this one—but luckily, it had turned up right when I'd needed it.

Still chewing, I shut the drawer and headed to the bathroom. It was tiny and cramped, but the water was blessedly hot.

The shower didn't clear my mind, but by the time I stepped out, there was noise from the main room below. I dressed quickly, once again in more serviceable jeans and a leather jacket, then headed down toward the noise.

The main room of our tower was a smaller version of the one at the shifters' tower. We used it as a central gathering space, and there was even a huge wooden chair by the fire for our leader, Carrow. She never sat in it, however. She might have, but her familiar, a fat raccoon named Cordelia, often snagged it before she could.

When I reached the room, that was the first thing I spotted—Cordelia, fat bum in the chair, her little paw shoved into a bag of Monster Munch. My own furry little stalker was nowhere to be seen, however.

The rest of our guild was gathered in the main part

of the room, sitting around a long table piled with pizza, papers, and books. Carrow, Mac, Quinn, Seraphia, and even Beatrix, our newest member, all turned to face me.

"Well?" Mac asked. "You clear your name yet?"

I shook my head. "Worse. I think the killer just tried to attack me while I was in the middle of town. Shoved me into the alley."

Carrow jumped up. "Someone tried to kill you?"

"Abduct me, I think." I shivered. "I fought him off, and he disappeared through a transport charm."

"Bloody hell." Mac dragged her hand through her short hair. "Do you have any idea why?"

"Not a clue in the world. But I'm going to find out." I looked at the stuff spread over the table. "What's all this?"

Carrow held up a book. "This is everything we could find that might help you. But it seems you need a bodyguard instead."

I joined them at the table, sitting next to Mac and grabbing a slice of still-hot pepperoni pizza. "How so?"

"The Alpha won't let us anywhere near you to help, so we collected everything we could locate about the shifters so that we could maybe find who might be after one of them."

Warmth exploded inside my chest, followed immediately by guilt. They were the best friends in the world, and I was *still* lying to them. I shoved the pizza in my mouth. It didn't work as well as a candy bar, unfortunately.

"Uh oh," Mac said. "What are you stressed about? More than just the murder?"

How the hell was she so insightful?

"The murder," I said around a too-big bite.

*That's all. Just the murder.*

I was going to have to come clean soon. But when?

"Here's what we've found." Carrow leaned forward. "Some of these folks vaguely remember this, but obviously, it was all new to me."

"Just spit it out," Mac said. "Apparently, Lachlan, the current Alpha, had to kill his father to protect the pack."

"He had to *what*?" I'd avoided all news of the pack ever since I'd returned to town, but that one was a real doozy.

"Yeah." Mac nodded. "No one speaks of it because it sucked so badly at the time. The old Alpha went wacko. Mad as a hatter. And it was up to Lachlan to put him down."

Holy fates. *That* was unexpected.

~

*Lachlan*

. . .

My heart thundered as I strode in the direction of the side of our guild tower, veering toward the cemetery. Fortunately, the courtyard was mostly empty, and no one stopped me.

I reached the cemetery and approached the huge old oak that grew at the side. Magic glittered around the tree, which acted as a portal between our place in Guild City and our ancestral lands in Scotland.

Everyone in the pack—from the smallest cat to the largest wolf—came to this tree to reach the Highlands and run. Living in Guild City was fine as long as we could get out and be free.

I strode straight into the portal at the base of the tree, letting the ether sweep me up and spin me through space. It spat me out in the fresh, brisk wind of a Highland afternoon. The sun shone brightly through the space in a thick white cloud, illuminating the rolling hills and tall mountains that were our home.

I breathed deeply.

I'd come here with my father as a boy, long before the curse had taken him. They'd been good times. I'd first shifted here. Raced with my brother here.

Damn, I missed him.

Inside, my wolf howled, desperate to be let free. It wanted to run, to chase, to hunt. I let it out far too infrequently, and it was getting anxious. I felt restless deep in my bones, almost an ache.

I longed for more than just running. I longed for the

past, when my father and brother were still here. Before everything fell apart.

I shook away the thoughts and headed toward the stone circle near the river. We owned thousands of acres in this desolate part of Scotland, but no one lived here except for our most revered seer. Her cottage was hidden, though, and one had to earn entry.

As I approached the standing stones that soared toward the sky, I felt the hum of their magic deep in my soul. There were thirteen of them, all nearly identical in shape and size.

I stepped through the ring and stopped in front of the stone basin situated directly in the middle of the circle. Quickly, I drew a blade from my pocket and made a small slice across my palm. Pain pinched, and the blood flowed freely. I let it drip into the basin before clenching my fist tightly and returning the blade to my pocket.

In the stone bowl, my blood sizzled and smoked. Magic would detect if I was one of the pack, and when it did, the seer's cottage would appear.

*If* she were willing.

I looked up toward the river about a hundred meters away. When the air began to shimmer, I felt a grim smile stretch across my face.

I was in luck.

I strode from the stone circle, heading toward the small cottage that was appearing at edge of the river.

Mountains sloped up on the far bank, dotted with fluffy white sheep that would need to get a move on before the next full moon.

As I walked toward the cottage, I reached into my pocket and retrieved the claw. It dug into my hand where I clutched it.

*All black eyes.*

A sign of the Darkest Moon curse.

There were a few wolves in the world who had it, but which of them would attack us? And which would keep a gruesome talisman like this? It was the entire claw, from root to tip. That could only be obtained by cutting it out of the wolf's foot, which would be hard as hell to do while a wolf was alive.

I reached my destination and pounded on the door. "It's your Alpha."

A few moments later, the door swung open, revealing an older woman with silver hair and bright green eyes. She was ageless, as far as I could tell, without a line on her face. Her hair fell in a waterfall down her back, gleaming brilliantly against her purple dress.

Agnes was the most powerful seer in our pack's history, with a particularly gifted ability for seeing into the past and future of the pack.

"Alpha." Her brows rose. "What can I do for you?"

"May I come in?"

She nodded and stepped back, letting me into her cottage. It was a small space, decorated with too many frilly cushions and pillows. The scent of incense hung heavy in the air, making my nose itch. Fortunately, I wouldn't be here long.

As soon as she shut the door, I turned and held out the claw. "I need to know who this belongs to. And which shifter killed Danny."

"You know I tried to see the answer to the second question already."

"This might give you more to go on."

"True." She frowned, looking at the claw. "But I'm not overly hopeful."

"Just try, please."

"Of course." She held out her hand and took the claw, gasping as her palm closed around it. Immediately, her gaze flew to mine. "It belonged to your father."

Head spinning, I stared at her. "My father. You're sure?"

"I am. I've never been surer of anything."

He couldn't be the murderer. I'd killed him myself, and the deed still haunted me. We'd laid him to rest in the pack crypt almost immediately after—in his wolf form.

Had someone desecrated the grave? And why?

Suddenly, the seer's eyes went dark, and her face went slack.

"Are you well?" I asked.

She blinked, her eyes clearing. All the color rushed from her face. "No. There's been another murder."

**12**

---

*Eve*

When I returned to the shifters' turf later that night, everything seemed different. Weird.

For one, the courtyard was completely empty. It was an hour when at least a couple people should have been going out to dinner or sitting at one of the open-air cafés on the square, yet it was dead silent.

I crossed the courtyard, nerves singing through me. The tower loomed overhead, every window blazing bright. I could see people hurrying back and forth behind the glass, never standing still.

*Something is wrong.*

When I got to the main steps and started to climb, the air felt electric. I'd just reached for the door when

Lachlan appeared at my elbow, having come around from the side so swiftly and quietly that I jumped.

I turned to him, surprised to see the shadows beneath his eyes and the grim lines bracketing his mouth. "Lachlan! What's going on?"

"There's been another murder."

Horror shot though me. "What? When?"

"Just a few hours ago today." His gaze moved to the scrape on my cheek, and he frowned. "What happened?"

"The killer attacked me. At least, I thought it was him. When I was walking back to my place, he grabbed me." I told him the whole story. "Do you think he failed with me and came here?"

"He may have."

"Damn it." Guilt streaked through me. "I should have fought harder. Chased him faster."

"No." His voice was sharp. "That's too dangerous. Why did he attack you?"

"I have no idea, and I didn't get anything that Alia didn't tell us already. Tall, like you. Dark eyes. Hood covered his face."

"Come with me." He gripped my arm and pulled me around the side of the building.

I followed, hurrying to keep up so that he didn't yank me off my feet. I thought he just might.

"Was it poison?" I asked. "Who was killed?"

He said nothing, just dragged me up the stairs and

pulled me right back into the bedroom he'd put me in before. At the door, he turned to look at me. "For fates' sake, don't leave this room, or you'll answer to me. There will be six guards on the door to protect you. You can't get past them, and no one can get in here."

I swallowed hard, the coldness in his voice sending shivers down my spine.

*Shit, shit, shit.*

He left, shutting the door behind him. I heard a lock click.

What the hell was I supposed to do now? He couldn't just keep me here.

At least it was the bedroom, and not the dungeons. I could fly out the window, but did I want to do that right now?

*Maybe not.*

Two shifters had been killed. The pack blamed me for the first. If they blamed me for the second as well, I couldn't let myself be caught by them. Not without Lachlan by my side. Shifters were hotheaded, full of emotion. I could fight with the best of them, but I didn't *want* to fight a bunch of people who were grieving a loss.

The other option was to fly out the window and go home. But what would that get me? I'd be farther from the action, and it was already nighttime.

I went to the window to see if I could spot anything outside. Surely something was happening out there.

With shaking hands, I unlocked the latch and pulled

it open. Immediately, I felt the difference from before. A protective charm now barred the window, put there to keep me from flying out again.

Damn it.

They really were keeping me prisoner. In nicer accommodation, but still, a prisoner. I spun around and went to the door, trying it even though I knew it was locked. I had a few potions that could burn through the metal, but now wasn't the time.

I needed a plan.

I turned back to the window, then stumbled away, surprised.

There, sitting on the ledge, was that damned raccoon.

He grinned toothily, his bandit mask dark against his pale gray face. He held out an Aero bar.

Surprise flashed through me. "What's that?"

He waggled the chocolate, clearly offering it.

"It's for me?" I approached slowly, unable to help the smile that stretched across my face.

He shoved the bar through the protective barrier, yanking his little hand back as soon as the magic sparked his fingers. The candy fell to the floor, and I picked it up. "Thank you."

But why the hell had he brought me a candy bar?

*You've had a bad day.*

My eyebrows shot upward. "Can you read my mind? Are you psychic?"

*No, I'm Ralph.*

Ralph. I could hear him inside my head, which meant he had to be my familiar. Carrow had one, too. Only she and her mate, Gray, could hear hers.

Why was I suddenly getting a familiar?

"How long have you been following me?" I asked.

He shrugged. *Don't know. You didn't need me until now.*

"I needed you to stop stealing my candy bars."

*'Fraid I can't do anything about that.*

He wasn't even going to try, but I wasn't about to argue. "What are you doing here?"

*Here to help break you out of the pokey.*

"I'm not sure I should leave just yet." An idea flashed. "Could you do a little recon, maybe?" I needed to find out what had happened to the victim. Guilt at the idea that he was dead because I hadn't stopped the killer nagged at me.

*You sure you want to stay? Hard to get chocolate bars when you're locked up.*

"I need answers. And as much as I want to charge out there and get them, it's a tower full of shifters who will be happy to tear me apart before I can get any. But *you*, on the other hand, are perfect for the job."

He preened. *I am very sneaky. But I'll require payment.* His gaze fell to the candy bar in my hand.

I sighed. "You just gave this to me."

*It's the thought that counts. Now give it back.*

Reluctantly, I did. "Be careful."

*They don't know I'm with you. Anyway, it's the Shifters' Guild. I'll fit in great.*

He disappeared, and I watched him scamper away along the wall, then down a chimney, straight into the belly of the tower.

I leaned back.

I had a familiar, and he was out there doing recon for me. True, he had waged a war of sweets-stealing terror against me, but he was helping me now.

Not so bad, overall.

The next hour passed at a glacial pace. Every five minutes, I debated trying to break through the barrier on the window to escape, but I didn't have the tools I needed. Anyway, Ralph was my best bet.

Finally, he scampered back up to the window and sat on the sill. It was full dark, and he looked like a little bandit.

"Well?" I asked.

*Not poison. A blade, straight across the throat of a shifter named Bill MacDougal. Everyone seemed to like him a whole lot, not like Danny. They're all really sad.*

Sorrow hit me.

Bill MacDougal. I remembered his name. Even his face. A nice guy with sharp cheekbones and a flop of dark hair. Hadn't he been friends with Lachlan and Garreth?

Damn, that sucked. My heart ached for Lachlan. For all of Bill's family and friends.

"Anything else?"

*They're planning a memorial for tonight.*

"Already?"

*They won't bury the body yet. Just an hour in honor of him. And the other guy. Shifters are an emotional lot. You know how it is.*

I did, though Lachlan definitely disproved that rule.

"Thanks for your help, Ralph." I frowned, thinking. "Could you do me one more favor?"

He nodded. *I know where to find payment.*

He had to mean my stash, but at this point, I'd buy him a ticket to Willy Wonka's chocolate factory. "In my workshop, near the back wall, there are rows of potion ingredients in glass bottles. A yellow one labeled *Mercanthia* should help me break the barrier on this window."

*On it, boss.* Ralph saluted, then turned and scampered down the wall.

My mind spun as I waited for him, never leaving my post at the window. A few shifters passed by, but the courtyard stayed mostly empty.

At one point, the door behind me opened. I spun around to see a tray get shoved inside, and then the door slammed shut and locked.

Lachlan.

It hadn't been him, but I was sure the food had come by his orders. Feeding me, but still keeping me locked up. I grabbed a sandwich to eat while I waited at the window, and I'd just taken my first bite when Ralph reappeared.

His eyes went right to my sandwich and gleamed.

"Let me guess, more payment required?"

He nodded.

"Push the potion through, and it's yours. *Half* of it."

He grinned, then set the potion on the wide stone sill and pushed it through the barrier, hissing when his fingertips touched it. We were lucky that things could pass through, even if people couldn't.

Quickly, I took the bottle and opened it, then deposited a thin line of the powder all along the windowsill. Once it was in place, I shooed Ralph away. He scampered to the side, and I blew on it, sending a cloud of dust into the invisible barrier.

It sparked brightly, and I grinned. "All good."

Ralph jumped back onto the windowsill and came through. I gave him half the sandwich, and we sat at the window, watching the shifters set up for the ceremony to come.

*Lachlan*

I watched from the back, my skin itching, as Bill's family and friends spoke words of memory at the front of the crowd. Every inch of me itched, in fact. I couldn't stand still.

The ceremony was necessary. Not just for the purpose of grieving, which plenty of people were doing, but because I wanted everyone in one place at one time. I'd spent all evening interviewing anyone who'd been near the tower, and I'd come up with nothing. This was my chance to speak to the entire pack without arousing suspicion. None of them would like the idea that I might suspect one of our own.

But *two* members of my pack had been murdered, and Bill's murder took it to the next level. Beyond the fact that he was well liked, he'd been killed in his flat inside our tower.

The method had been different than the one that had taken Danny, but two murders in such a short time had to be connected.

Who the hell had slipped in?

Just an hour ago, I'd had confirmation from contacts out in Guild City that they'd seen Eve walking toward our tower at the time of the murder, escorted by all of her friends. She was in the clear—of that, at least.

Her other secrets? I was more determined than ever to get to the bottom of them.

Worry tugged at me. The killer had attacked her. Why? Did it have to do with whatever she was hiding?

The idea of her at risk scared the hell out of me.

*Nothing can happen to her.*

The depth of my fear for her was unnatural. I shouldn't care this much. I shouldn't care at all.

I shook my head, trying not to think of her.

I needed this time—totally undistracted by her—to look for signs of guilt, worry, or fear. Not just in faces, but in body language and scent. It was a long shot, but I was willing to take it.

Soon, the ceremony was over, and people began to mingle. I joined them, trying to keep a clear head as I spoke. The others' grief began to rub me raw, forcing memories to the surface.

Danny and Bill had been my brother's friends when we'd been young. *My* friends. Bill had stayed a decent guy, and now he was dead. Just like Garreth. Just like Danny.

Was I next?

I hoped so.

I'd love for the bastard to come after me.

But no. There wasn't a connection between the three deaths. Garreth had died years ago in a car accident. I'd seen his body, broken on the side of the road, before the paramedics took him away. I'd *buried* him, for fates's sake. Not like Danny or Bill. And those two hadn't been friends in years.

I dragged a hand through my hair, hating the feeling in my chest. It shouldn't be there. The potion should have banished all emotion, but lately, it wasn't working very well. I reached for the flask in my pocket and took a swig, enjoying the burn. When that still didn't work, I drank more, wishing I could get drunk. It was a weak thing to want, especially given that I was the Alpha.

I shook my head and turned to search the crowd for anyone that I hadn't spoken to today. I found a few and approached, subtly using my ability to command the truth from them to determine where they'd been when Bill had been killed.

I hated that I was questioning my own pack members. It made my stomach turn. There was still a chance it was an outside job, but the fact that Bill had been killed in the tower...

Fates, I hated this.

All around me, people grieved. Each tear felt like a slice to my skin, and eventually, I couldn't take it anymore. I grabbed a whisky bottle from the refreshments table and left, needing to find a quiet spot. I had spent so much of my life not feeling, but somehow, in the space of days, the potion that had worked for so long was failing me.

*Eve.*

It was her fault. It had to be.

But how? How the hell could a fae make me feel this way? I hadn't felt this way since I'd seen the girl fate had chosen for me. My mate.

Eve wasn't my mate. She was fae.

*Unless she's not fae.*

The thought struck me as I strode toward the cemetery behind the row of shops and restaurants that bordered the courtyard.

No, that was ridiculous. I'd seen her use fae magic. It was no simple glamour.

But what if she was capable of more than a simple glamour?

The thought was crazy. I'd never heard of anyone accomplishing that sort of magic, and my Alpha's Command hadn't worked on her. She wasn't a shifter.

I shook my head, frustration and worry dogging at my heels.

The Dark Moon curse was coming for me. I could feel it.

## 13

*Eve*

I watched the memorial from my window, keeping my gaze on Lachlan the entire time. He mingled in the crowd, speaking to some people and watching others like a hawk. Occasionally, he sipped from the ever-present flask in his pocket.

It was all normal—exactly what one would expect in such a circumstance. Perhaps the memorial was happening a bit quickly, considering that the murder had been less than twelve hours ago, but that wasn't unheard of.

From the way Lachlan made the rounds, I had to assume he was looking for people who seemed suspicious. He was too clever and too driven not to be using this opportunity.

But he seemed...off. There was something about the set of his shoulders and the glint in his eyes. He was being weird. I didn't know him well, but that damned connection between us was impossible to ignore. There was something not quite right about him now.

When he grabbed a full whisky bottle and headed away from the crowd, I made my decision.

Carefully, I climbed out the window and crept along the roof. If someone looked for me, they'd see me, but it was better than being all flashy with my wings. Finally, I reached a quiet spot where I could fly down to the side of the tower. I hurried through the dark, headed to the old cemetery.

I found Lachlan sitting on a bench next to his brother's grave. He just sat there, staring into the distance, the whisky bottle held loosely in his hand.

He looked so...broken.

I stopped nearby, and he glanced at me.

"Doing all right?" I asked.

"Fine." He frowned. "What are you doing out of your room? It's dangerous."

"It seemed like it was time."

"I shouldn't be surprised you didn't stay put."

"Not really my style." I eyed the bottle. It was half empty, and I swore it had been full when I'd seen him take it. Yet he showed no sign of inebriation. "How much have you had?"

"A lot more than this." He took a swig. "Doesn't do much, though."

"Then why drink it?"

"I like the burn, and I need to kill some time." He looked back at me. "You need to be more careful and not wander around at night. What are you doing here, Eve?"

*Checking on you.* But I couldn't say that. It also wasn't the entire truth. "I want to know what's going on. Why are you killing time?"

"A band will start soon. Shifters can't resist a band. Once it starts, everyone will be distracted, and I'll be able to check my father's crypt without letting anyone know. If it's been desecrated, I don't want anyone seeing it."

*His father's crypt.*

No wonder he was drinking. Even if the booze didn't do much to him, I'd be drinking, too. "Why do you need to check his crypt?"

He drew in a low, tortured breath. "That claw was my father's. I buried him in wolf form. Intact."

*Shit.*

He was psyching himself up to check on the probably-desecrated grave of the father he'd had to kill. I drew in a shuddery breath. "How do you know?"

"The seer."

Of course. The shifters' seer was powerful.

"Do you know what happened to my father?" he asked.

"Not the whole story." There had to be more to it. A reason. A good one.

"The Dark Moon curse took him."

I frowned. "What's that?"

He stared up at the sky. "Something that haunts the wolves of various packs. Not just ours. Though we've been particularly unlucky to have lost an Alpha to it." He paused a moment, then continued. "Shifters feel emotions particularly strongly."

*Don't I know it.* "I've heard."

"Well, a few of us feel them so strongly that they eventually drive us mad. We lose control over our wolf form. Worse, we lose our loyalty to our pack. We become loose cannons, violent and unstable, and eventually go feral."

"Shit." No one had ever mentioned this to me when I was a kid. Wasn't exactly the stuff of bedtime stories. "And that's what happened to your father?"

He nodded. "When I was eighteen."

That's how old he'd been when we'd formally met. My own mother had died that same year. I'd thought no one could have a worse year than I'd had. I'd been wrong.

"And you had to kill him to save everyone else," I guessed.

"It's shifter law to put down those who've fallen to

the curse." He gave a bitter laugh. "Anyway, it was the humane thing to do. For everyone." He held up the flask that sat next to him on the bench. "And this is supposed to keep me from feeling anything."

"It's not just whisky, then?"

"No, it's not. But it's not working anymore." He rose and approached me. "It stopped working when you appeared."

I stiffened and looked up at him, my heart racing. His dark eyes burned into me, tracing over my face. Over my lips. Tension sparked the air between us, and I had the most insane urge to press my hands to his chest. To pull him down to me so that I could kiss him.

"What is it about you?" he whispered, his voice rough. "*Why* has everything changed? You're fae—you shouldn't be able to do this to me."

Something like hurt pierced me through the heart. Was it because I was pretty now? We'd always had the mate bond—according to fate, at least—but he shouldn't be able to feel it as long as I wore my enchanted necklace. So was it because I'd grown out of my ugly duckling state?

As much as I wanted him now, I couldn't forget the words he'd once hurled at me. We'd both been young, but the wound had been real. And I didn't want to be suckered into being his mate, especially when it could end with my death. No guy was worth dying over.

I stepped back, my mind racing. "It's timing, that's all. Stressful with the murders. It's your imagination."

Shadows flickered across his eyes, and he nodded. I was sixty-five percent sure he didn't believe me, but there was nothing else I could say.

Fortunately, the band chose that moment to start playing.

Lachlan's smile turned grim. "I can go check my father's crypt now."

I nodded. "I'm coming with you."

He gave me a long look, and it was clear as day that he wanted to say no. Instead, he gave a sharp nod.

I followed him through the cemetery, heading toward the mausoleums at the back. There was one for each previous Alpha, the most impressive buildings in the cemetery. As we walked, wind rustled through the trees, and the moonlight scattered on the ground at our feet. The tombstones almost glowed beneath the light, beautiful and solemn. The whole place was lovely, almost, which was strange to say about a cemetery on the same day that a packmate had died. An owl hooted, and it sounded like an admonishment.

As we walked, I asked, "Bill, the victim. Were there any clues?"

His gaze flashed over to mine. "How do you know his name?"

"I had a friend do a little recon."

He frowned, anger flashing in his eyes.

"Not a person," I said hurriedly, knowing he wouldn't like the idea of my friends sneaking around his tower. Guilds infiltrating each other's towers was *very* frowned upon. "A raccoon."

"A raccoon? They shouldn't even live in London."

"I know. Doesn't stop Ralph, though. But I don't want to talk about him. I want to talk about finding the killer." I gripped his arm, and he stiffened.

I'd forgot how opposed to touch he was. He'd cut himself off from it for so long, according to the cook I'd spoken to.

He pulled away, his breathing sharp.

I flexed my hand, feeling the burn of his flesh still imprinted into my palm. My words were rough as they escaped my throat. "What about Bill?"

He seemed to exert a conscious effort to rein himself in. "The dark eyes that the apothecary mentioned are a sign of the Dark Moon curse. Whoever is killing my pack has it."

*Shit.* "The poisoning took planning. But if the killer is going mad, changing weapons makes sense. He no longer has the control he once had."

"That's my thought."

"And it could be a shifter from any pack?"

He nodded. "I'm putting out word to the other packs, asking if they've lost anyone to it recently. Why they'd target us, I don't know."

"We'll figure it out." If his father's grave really had been disturbed, that could be a big clue.

We'd reached the mausoleum at the back of the cemetery, right at the base of the looming city wall. Moonlight gleamed on it like a spotlight, almost as if the fates knew exactly where we were headed.

*We're going to find something here.*

The thought was so eerie that it sent a shiver across my skin. I ignored it and focused on the scene, trying to pick up any clues. It was an impressive structure, about three meters by four, if I had to guess. Carved with ornate swirls and inset with marble, it was definitely the nicest one here.

Had it been Lachlan who'd done that? In guilt over his father's death?

He stopped about two meters from the entrance and knelt to inspect the ground. "No tracks. No recent scent."

"May I approach the door?" I asked.

He nodded and stood, following me.

The huge stone slab that acted as a door seemed to be slightly off kilter, like it had been moved aside and put back in a rush.

"Someone has been here," he said.

I shivered, imagining them prying the heavy door off to reach the body inside.

Carefully, Lachlan gripped either side of the door and lifted it, moving it to the left. The thing had to weigh two or three hundred kilograms, but he picked it up like it was nothing.

"Whoever broke in had to be strong," I said, as he gently leaned the slab against the wall.

He just grunted.

The interior of the mausoleum was pitch black, so I withdrew my mobile and turned on the torch. When I shone it inside, I gasped.

The place was a mess. The stone sarcophagus inside had been smashed to bits, and bones were scattered through the room. I couldn't even tell if his father had been buried as a wolf or a man.

Anger vibrated in Lachlan's voice. "The killer didn't just take the claw."

I shivered as I stared at the scene. Rage seemed to permeate the space, as if the shattered stone and scattered bones told a story of unimaginable anger.

"Oh, no," I breathed.

Slowly, he walked inside, careful to avoid any of the disturbed interior. "I can't smell whoever was here, and it doesn't look like anything was left behind."

I followed him in, sticking close to the wall near the door. I didn't want to destroy any of the evidence, even though I wasn't sure what I was looking for.

A business card with his name and address on it, ideally.

But there was nothing unusual in the place besides the destruction and the weird feeling in the air. There was no scent remaining, but I swore I could feel the attacker's rage. It turned my stomach.

I looked at Lachlan, catching sight of the shadows in his eyes. His jaw was tight with anger, but his eyes...they looked sad. My heart twisted.

"Come on," I said. "We need to make a plan. It's clear there's nothing to find in here right now, so we need to determine what to do next."

He nodded, and I could see the anger in the tightness of his jaw and the sharpness of the gesture. His sadness was being swallowed by his rage.

I waited as he carefully replaced the door, and we retreated to a tree a dozen meters away. Lachlan walked quickly, as if he didn't want to stand too close to his father's desecrated body. We stopped beneath the thick, leafy branches that cut out the moonlight, lingering in the shadows.

He took another swig from his flask as I stared at the mausoleum, my mind racing. "When I was at a party thrown by the Witches' Guild, they mentioned a sorceress who could recreate scenes of the past, as long as they happened in a cemetery. Something about the spirits of the dead providing enough energy for her to rewind time."

"Mariketta." Lachlan nodded. "I know her."

"Let's get her here. She can recreate the moment the crypt was broken into. Maybe we'll see our guy. Or girl."

He nodded, his gaze thoughtful. "That's good. We'll do that."

"I can get her contact info."

But he was already reaching for his mobile and dialing. I watched, breath held, as he spoke to someone on the other end of the line. It didn't take long for him to hang up and look at me. "I need to go speak with her. You're coming with me. I don't want you out of my sight."

I nodded, my heart thumping.

I needed to get the hell out of his sight. For my own good, as well as for his. But that wouldn't be happening right now. And anyway, I wanted to know what this sorceress found. "Where is she? Her guild tower?"

"No. She's at the Orpheus Theater and refuses to leave. We need to meet her there."

"The theater?" I frowned, looking down at my apparel. "Will they even let me in, looking like this?"

"We'll manage."

We left the cemetery in silence, exiting via the side instead of the front in order to avoid the crowd of shifters still mourning Bill and Danny. I could hear people dancing and singing, and shouts of "Bill!" as we passed.

Lachlan led the way expertly through the quiet city streets, and we reached the theater about ten minutes later. Sparkling lights over the door advertised that Cirque was in town. Maybe if this all went south for me,

I could join up and travel the world with them. Not that I had any fire breathing or acrobat skills, but I'd manage.

The usher at the door gave me a disdainful look as we approached, but he wiped it from his face as soon as Lachlan glared at him. The Alpha wasn't properly attired, either, but that apparently didn't matter.

"Welcome." The usher bowed and opened the door.

Lachlan inclined his head and strode inside. I followed, eyes on the ground. Generally, I respected dress codes, especially for fancy places, since it was the easiest way to blend in.

The main lobby, all done up in red velvet and bright gilt, was empty, but the roar of the crowd could be heard from behind the lobby wall.

"Do you know where she sits" I asked.

"Box 215."

I nodded. All of the boxes should be on the upper level.

Together, we approached the massive staircase. A velvet rope blocked our path, but we ducked underneath the barrier to ascend. Only the cream of Guild City's society got a box at the top of the theater. Lachlan would have qualified due to his wealth and power. I didn't qualify in any kind of way.

We climbed the red-carpeted stairs silently and quickly. At the top, a simple, wide hallway stretched behind the boxes—empty, thank fates.

Lachlan turned right, following the tiny signs on the

walls, and I hurried to keep up. We were approximately halfway to her box when Lachlan hesitated, tilting his head slightly.

"Do you hear something?" I asked.

"Torin, leader of the fae guild." He veered a sharp right toward a tiny door set in the back wall, and I followed. "I can smell the bastard from a mile away, and he's about to turn that corner in front of us. We have bad blood, and you're not in his guild, when you very likely should be. We can't afford a scene right now."

He was right about that. Torin loved a scene, and these boxes were ticketed only. Not to mention that I'd pissed Torin off when I'd chosen to join the Shadow Guild instead of the Fae Guild. He might not start anything, but we didn't have time to waste.

Lachlan gripped the handle of a little door next to where we stood, but it didn't budge. He yanked hard, breaking the lock. We slipped inside the tiny, dark closet, and he shut it behind us.

Immediately, his scent wrapped around me, woodsy and clean. I tried to breathe shallowly to keep my chest from pressing against his, but it was no use. The damned place was so tiny that we brushed against each other from chest to knee. Heat burned into me, making my head spin. This was only the third time we'd made contact, and the feel of it was intoxicating. Every inch of me vibrated.

Hiding in this closet no longer felt like an easy way

to avoid a delay. Instead, it had turned into a high-stakes game of seven minutes in heaven.

Silly. There was no way he'd kiss me.

When I heard him inhale slightly, clearly scenting me, surprise flashed through me. That was very lupine.

I looked up at him, unable to help myself.

I could barely see him through the dark, and it wrapped us in a cocoon.

When he spoke, his voice was rough. "What is it about you?"

My breath caught in my throat. "You already asked me that."

But it didn't sound the same that time. There was desire thick in his voice. I felt it wrap around me, supernaturally strong, and pull me toward him. My head went woozy with it, and suddenly, it was hard to breathe.

He raised a hand to my face, cupping my jaw. His skin burned against mine, an electric heat that made my heart race and warmth flush through me.

When he dipped his head into the crook of my neck and inhaled, every inch of me felt alive.

I knew I should jerk away—I couldn't risk him discovering my true scent. It was hidden by the potion that anointed my necklace, but eventually, he would recognize that I was his mate.

A low groan reverberated from his throat. "You smell amazing."

*Kiss me.*

It was the only thought in my head. All my rational thought had fled, driven away by our proximity, and I wanted to throw myself at him.

When he leaned down to hover his lips over mine, I moaned slightly, shifting to lean up on my toes.

Before we made contact, I must have brushed something against the wall behind us. A broom fell on my head, shocking me out of my trance. Cold doused me, and I jerked back, bumping into a bucket.

He stiffened, and we managed to find a scant inch of space between us.

"Torin is gone," he said.

"Good." I pushed the door open and slipped out, grateful to see that no one was in the hall.

I turned away from Lachlan, pressing my hands to my hot cheeks to drive back the chilly fear.

*What* had just happened?

I'd wanted to kiss him, sure, but *that* had been an otherworldly kind of desire. Not normal. I looked back at him, catching sight of the heat in his eyes and the confusion on his face.

I swallowed hard and looked forward. Something had definitely changed between us, as if touching that much had unlocked something inside our subconsciousness.

*No.* It couldn't be possible.

## 14

*Lachlan*

What the bloody hell had just happened?

I'd lost my goddamned mind in there. I hadn't been that close to a woman in years, and something about Eve had driven every ounce of sense from my head. I hadn't felt desire like that...ever. It was almost like touching her had ignited something. And her scent...

When I'd pressed my face to her neck, she'd smelled like heaven. And yet, she *hadn't* smelled like my mate. My wolf would have recognized her, and it hadn't. But how could she smell so good and *not* be my mate? Everything in me was starting to shout that she was.

But she couldn't be. She definitely wasn't the same

girl I'd met years ago. She wasn't even a shifter—she was a fae, for fates' sake.

It didn't matter that I wanted her more than I wanted my next breath, it was too dangerous.

I dragged a hand through my hair, trying to shove the thoughts from my mind. I was a mess from finding my father's crypt destroyed. His bones…

The sight still haunted me.

I was losing it, and my obsession with Eve was a manifestation of that. I'd think on it more when this was over. Until then, my focus needed to be entirely on finding the killer.

Finally, we reached Mariketta's box.

I knocked briefly, then slipped inside, Eve following behind me. The box was empty except for Mariketta, who wore a severe black gown and sparkling jewels. Everything about Mariketta screamed power, and I respected it.

Behind her, the circus flashed in a series of magnificent colors as acrobats leapt through the air.

She looked at me, a sly smile on her face. "You made it. Didn't run into Torin, did you?"

"You knew we might."

She shrugged, smiling. "Perhaps."

Meddling sorceress, always looking to cause trouble. No wonder she'd insisted we come here. She looked around my back, spotting Eve. "Well, now, who are you?"

"Eve. Shadow Guild."

Mariketta's eyebrows shot up. "The potion maker."

"The same." Eve took a seat next to Mariketta. I took the one behind, and the two women turned to face me, forming a small circle. "We're hoping you can help us turn back time in a cemetery."

Surprise flashed on Mariketta's face. "That's a difficult spell. A rare one. You're sure you need it?"

"We do," I said. "Can you do it?"

"Of course I can. The question is…will I?"

"What is your price?"

She pursed her lips, then smiled. "Money. A lot of it."

Thank fates. Something was going our way today. "How much?"

"Twenty thousand pounds." She watched me, and I probably should have flinched, because she added, "Thirty, actually."

Eve had turned pale, but I just nodded. "Thirty. And we do it as soon as possible."

"At dawn tomorrow, then. We'll need the energy of the rising sun."

I nodded. "Thank you."

"Your cemetery, I presume?"

"Aye. In the back, near the mausoleums."

She nodded, then looked more carefully at Eve and me. "There's something between you two."

Panic flashed in Eve's eyes. That was strange. I'd expect denial or annoyance, but panic?

"Thank you." I stood, deciding to ignore Mariketta's prodding.

Eve nodded gratefully to Mariketta, then raced from the box. I nodded goodbye and followed her out. We left the theater in silence, fortunate to avoid everyone as we exited.

"I'd like to sleep at my place tonight," Eve said.

"You'll sleep at the tower."

"I'm wearing this damned dog collar, Lachlan." Anger vibrated in her voice. "You can find me, no matter what, so the least you can do is let me sleep in my own bed."

"You'll sleep in the tower, and that's the last of it." I didn't want her far from me. It was ridiculous and dangerous, but I wanted her close by.

She huffed, then picked up the pace. We walked the entire way in silence, reaching the courtyard in front of my Guild tower without incident.

We were about to cross the street toward the courtyard when a noise sounded from a rooftop. I stiffened and looked up. A shadowy figured moved, just barely visible in the shadows.

A half second later, I heard the faintest pull of a metal trigger. The short bolt caught the moonlight as it hurtled toward us. *Crossbow.*

I recognized it immediately. It had once been a

favored weapon of mine.

I grabbed Eve and dove right, wrapping myself around her. The bolt thudded into the wall behind us.

"What happened?" Eve tried to scramble up.

"Take cover behind that bench."

It was close enough she could get behind it, and she did, moving fast. She crouched behind it and drew her bag from the ether. Quickly, she passed me a potion bomb and took one for herself.

From the roof, I could barely hear the sound of the attacker loading another bolt into his crossbow.

I pressed my comms charm. "Backup! Across the square!"

I stood and hurled the potion bomb at the roof. The attacker fired off the crossbow at the same time. I dove left but moved too slowly, and the bolt sliced through the outside edge of my arm just as the potion bomb slammed into the tiled roof. It exploded with a bang, sending a wave of force out.

Eve threw an identical second bomb, and another boom reverberated through the night.

"They might have knocked him out," she said, passing me a bomb.

I squinted up into the dark, catching sight of a brilliant cloud of silver powder poofing upward. "Damn it. Transport charm."

Panting, Eve slumped against the bench.

I knelt, inspecting her face. "Are you alright?"

"Me?" Her gaze went to my arm. "What about you."

"It's nothing. I got lucky."

"Why the hell is he after me?"

"I don't know. But we'll find out."

She nodded. "Let me go check the roof."

"It's too dangerous."

She scowled and shoved me, then stood and called upon her wings. She was airborne before I could stop her. Six of my security force arrived while she was on the roof, and we waited for her to finish. A few minutes later, she returned, shaking her head. "There's nothing up there."

"We'll know more in the morning. Come on."

We headed back to the tower, my guards leaving us when we stepped inside. I escorted her all the way up to her temporary bedroom. At the door, she turned back. "I'll meet you before dawn." I nodded, and she shut the door.

I stared at it for a long moment. Twice, now, she'd been attacked. Each time, I'd felt fear like I hadn't felt in years.

What was I going to do when we caught this killer? Let her go?

*Aye.*

I had to. This obsession was mad.

I scrubbed a hand through my hair and turned to leave, reaching for the flask in my back pocket. As I raised it to my lips, I realized that drinking was ridiculous. The potion wasn't working, and I needed something stronger.

I checked my watch. Midnight.

It would be daytime in Magic's Bend, Oregon, one of the largest all-supernatural cities in America. The blood sorceress who provided me with my potion didn't live in Guild City. That had been a conscious choice on my part. I liked the fact that she was halfway around the world. I didn't need my pack knowing that I relied on a potion to keep my emotions at bay.

Quickly, I strode to my quarters and let myself into the cold room. It was austere, which suited me, and I took the last of the two transport charms from the dresser in my bedroom. I'd need to replace them soon, but there was no other way to reach Oregon and get back before dawn.

I hurled one to the ground and envisioned the quiet street. A silver cloud burst upward, and I stepped inside, letting the ether suck me in and spin me through space. It spat me out on a street corner in Darklane, the dark magic district of Magic's Bend. The supernaturals who lived and worked there weren't necessarily evil, but the magic they used walked the line between good and bad.

Victorian-era houses rose tall on either side of the street, their wooden fronts and ornate trim covered in the grime of dark magic. The entire place was dark gray from it, and even the sun seemed to shine less brightly on this street.

I spotted the sign that swung over a once-purple building a few houses down: *The Apothecary's Jungle.* Quickly, I strode toward it, taking the steps two at a time. I knocked hard, waiting impatiently. A few minutes later, the door creaked open. A woman in a black silk bathrobe with a sweep of black eye makeup stared out at me, her hair piled onto her head in a bouffant so big that it should have its own post code. I'd once thought she was beautiful, but now the only person I could see in my head was Eve.

"Mordaca. Just who I'm looking for."

"Lachlan." She scowled, her blood-red lips twisting in annoyance. "It's godawful early, you know that?"

"It's four p.m."

"Like I said." She turned and gestured for me to follow, flashing black nails that had been filed into points. "But come in. It must be important."

She led me through a dark hallway to a workshop dominated by an enormous table in the middle and a hearth on one side. She glided around the table to lean against the shelves decorating the opposite wall, crossing her arms over her chest to stare at me.

"The potion you've given me is no longer working," I said. "Does it expire?"

She laughed. "It's not milk. It doesn't expire." She frowned. "But it shouldn't stop working, either."

"Can you make a stronger one?"

"First, I want to understand why it's stopped working. What changed? What did you do?"

"Nothing." I hesitated. "A woman showed up."

Her eyebrows rose. "Oh."

"She means nothing to me."

"My potion begs to differ." She tapped her fingernails against her chin, clearly thinking. "That potion is meant to suppress all emotions. But whatever you feel for her...well, it's strong. Does it feel strong?"

"It feels strange." I didn't even know what strong emotion felt like anymore. "Perhaps I just want her."

She shrugged. "It's possible. Desire isn't quite the same as other emotions. It's physical as well as mental. So it could be breaking through the potion. If you've been celibate all this time..."

She eyed me up and down, and I just nodded.

"Well, maybe that's it. You should just sleep with her and get it out of your system. Then maybe you'll go back to normal."

The idea made my blood race. I wanted that, but I couldn't have it. "That's not going to happen."

"She married?"

"It's just not going to happen. Can you give me something stronger?"

She sighed. "Yeah. I can try to give you something with more kick. No promises, though."

*No promises.*

Bloody hell.

*Eve*

Before dawn, I woke in my room in the Shifters' Guild tower. For a half second, I stared at the ceiling, letting last night play through my mind.

Something had changed at the theater.

I'd felt his gaze on me the entire walk back, but we hadn't spoken a word.

Memories of our near kiss flashed through my mind. One more of those, and he'd be on to me. It wasn't logical, but I could feel it in my gut. I was running out of time before he figured out that I was not as I seemed.

Lachlan was too clever. And even though it was supposed to be impossible to change species, it clearly wasn't. He was going to figure it out.

I didn't want to be here when he did.

I shivered and dressed quickly. Dawn was coming, and I didn't want to miss the meeting with the sorceress. While I'd slept, someone had delivered a fresh set of underwear and socks.

I stared at them piled in the chair, horror flashing through me.

*They were mine.*

Lachlan hadn't sent a shifter into my guild tower, had he? That would be totally unforgivable.

*Don't get your knickers in a twist, it wasn't him.*

I turned, searching for the voice. Ralph sat on the windowsill, grinning at me. The little raccoon held a Cadbury bar in his small hand.

"Did you bring me those?"

He nodded. *Think of me as your butler. You know how to pay me.*

I looked between him and the underthings, imaging him running through the street, clutching my pants. Worse, they were my oldest pair, reserved only for laundry day. "I'm going to need half your chocolate bar."

He grumbled, but I heard him plop down off the windowsill and click-clack his way to me. He handed up half the candy bar, and I shoved it in my mouth.

I was going to need a lot more than that. "Thanks, mate."

I hadn't got the clean clothes in the most ideal way, but I was glad to have them.

*See you.* He shoved the last of the chocolate into his mouth and scampered up the windowsill, his fat bum taking a few extra heaves to get going. He disappeared into the night, and I dressed, then headed downstairs. Fortunately, I didn't run into anyone as I walked.

Lachlan waited for me in the main hall, standing near the exit. He looked every inch the powerful Alpha that he was, but there were shadows under his eyes that made me wonder where he'd spent the night.

I squared my shoulders and approached, making eye

contact. I made sure to hold it the whole way there, no matter how uncomfortable. At some point, I should have been forced to look away. He was the Alpha, and just like the Alpha's Command, there was magic in his gaze. No subordinate wolf should be able to hold his gaze for too long.

But the longer I held it, the easier it became.

That was weird, but maybe it was the necklace's doing. A fae shouldn't have any trouble holding his gaze.

"Good morning." He held out a paper-wrapped sandwich, and I could smell the eggs and bread. My stomach grumbled.

"Thank you." I took it, appreciating the gesture. He was always feeding me, though he looked kind of annoyed by it. Almost like he felt compelled to care, but he didn't want to.

"Dawn is coming." He turned toward the door. "Let's go."

I followed him out of the tower and across the quiet courtyard. Guild City was just beginning to wake up, and I could see movement behind the window of the coffee shop across the way. As much as I'd kill for a coffee, now wasn't the time.

The cemetery was silent as we entered, our footsteps disturbing the mist that hung low over the ground. The headstones watched us silently as we made our way toward the back. This morning, it was creepy. Nothing like last night.

As we walked, I kept a lookout for my mother's headstone. I hadn't visited it since her burial, though I'd often wanted to. But if I were caught here, how would I explain it?

The sorceress waited for us by the crypt. Today, she wore a simple black cloak and had her hair pulled up in a complicated knot atop her head. Severe black eyeliner and pale lipstick completed her look, and it was definitely cool.

She solemnly gazed at the two of us. "You're sure you want to do this?"

Lachlan nodded. "We need to know what happened here."

"All right. I'll turn back time as far as I can. It will be easier if it happened recently."

"I believe it did."

She nodded and reached into the large leather bag that hung over her arm. As the morning light turned pale gray, she removed large colored stones and placed them in a semicircle around the entrance of the crypt. I watched, intrigued, as she anointed each stone with oil from a tiny silver vial.

She looked at Lachlan. "If you'll remove the door now, we can get started."

He strode toward the crypt and lifted the stone without trouble, setting it aside so that it leaned against the wall.

"Thank you." She took her place directly across from

the entry to the mausoleum and gestured for us to stand behind her. We did as she asked, taking up a position that allowed us to see through the doorway into the crypt.

She removed her black gloves and dabbed some of the oil onto the backs of her hands, then tucked the silver vial away in her bag. As the first rays of sunlight began to turn the clouds pink, she raised her hands and began to chant. The language was unfamiliar—it didn't even sound modern, in fact.

Magic sparked on the air, coming from all around us.

I shivered. The graves—that had to be it.

Blue light began to glow from the ground, rising to the surface to gleam in the mist. The sorceress chanted louder, and the light rose up in arcs, traveling from the graves to the stones that she'd laid out. The brilliant blue light was almost blinding as it sliced through the air, forming a lattice dome around the entrance to the crypt.

When the sun shone directly onto the dome, the air popped, magic sparking so hard against my skin that I winced and stepped back. The glowing lattice faded, and a faint wind picked up. It blew straight across the walkway, and my head spun. It felt almost as if it were pushing time along.

The sorceress watched with bright eyes, continuing to chant.

When the shadowy, nearly transparent figure appeared, I jumped. "He's dressed the same as the guy who attacked me," I said. "Same size, too." Unfortunately, he was still wearing the hoodie that obscured his face.

Lachlan stepped around to the side, trying to get a better view, but judging by the frustration on his face, it didn't work. The man kept his head lowered and the hood carefully concealing his features. Lachlan stepped closer, as if he were going to cross the blue light barrier, but the sorceress gestured him back, murmuring, "Too dangerous."

His mouth tightened, but he nodded and stayed put.

The shadowy man strode toward the crypt and removed the stone door as easily as Lachlan had. Then he entered and stared at the coffin for one long moment. My heart lodged itself firmly in my throat as I watched him shove the lid off the sarcophagus. The stone slab fell to the floor and shattered.

The next moments were chaos. He lost his shit, smashing the sarcophagus to pieces, picking up slabs of stone and swinging them against the wall. The rage in his movements made me slightly nauseous. When he started to tear the skeleton apart, I felt my stomach really turn, and I flinched when the attacker threw the wolf skull right against the wall.

I glanced at Lachlan, hating the way his dark eyes were shadowed with pain. For someone who had avoided emotion for so long, he was really getting hit hard with it lately.

The spectacle continued for ten minutes, until I was desperate to ask the sorceress to end it. Instead, I bit my lip. We had to learn from this, and so I forced myself to watch, to search for any clue we might find.

Finally, the man exited the mausoleum. I caught sight of the wolf's claw clutched in his hand.

That bastard. It was a memento.

As he approached, I ducked low, trying to catch sight of his features. Unfortunately, he was extremely good at keeping his face tilted down. I could see nothing but the sweep of a pale nose and brilliant, dark eyes.

Entirely black.

Just like the apothecary had said. Just like I'd seen in the alley.

The Dark Moon curse.

No question. Especially with the way he'd destroyed the sarcophagus. The sheer madness of the act had been visible in every movement.

As he neared me, I searched his body frantically, looking for any kind of clue. Why couldn't he be wearing a free shirt from his accommodation, stating the name of the block of flats?

Of course he wasn't.

But his trousers...

The cuff of one of the legs of his jeans was rolled up slightly, the hem flipped as if it had caught on something. And there, tucked inside the denim, was a flower. It looked like it had got lodged there when he'd been striding through a garden bed. And damned if it wasn't distinct. Tall and slender, with brilliant red droplet-shaped petals—I'd never seen anything like it.

I knelt down and yanked my mobile from my pocket, determined to snap a picture.

"That won't work," the sorceress said. "Best memorize it."

I did as she commanded, using the next few precious seconds to commit the bloom to memory. I tried to store away every little detail. It was a flimsy clue, but I had to take it since no more were coming my way.

A moment later, the man stepped out of the magic circle and disappeared.

I heaved a sigh and looked down, praying that the flower would be enough.

Lachlan strode over to rejoin us. He thanked the sorceress and arranged payment. When she'd departed, I looked at him. "I'm going to try to find out what kind of flower was in the cuff of his trousers. Maybe it can lead us to a place he's been."

Lachlan nodded. "It's a long shot."

"What are you going to do?"

"I have a meeting with the Alphas of some of the other packs." He looked back at the mausoleum. "That was targeted. Whoever is killing people in our clan is extremely angry with my father."

"Did he have a lot of enemies?"

"A few. He was a hard man, intractable. And he spent a good bit of time before becoming Alpha on the security force at Glencarrough. I didn't think much of it before now, but he's clearly a linchpin in all of this."

No question.

I was just grateful that he wasn't commanding me to accompany him to Glencarrough. It was the headquarters of all shifters, located in Scotland. The security force there was a bit like a police force that made sure shifters followed the law. When someone did wrong against another pack, it was Glencarrough that stepped in. Only the strongest were on that security force, and Lachlan's father had been more than strong.

"He made enemies there, I imagine," I said.

"A few, probably." He nodded. "I'm going to find out who, and if any of them are out of prison now."

It wasn't a bad theory. In fact, it was the best one we had so far. "Good luck. I'll let you know if I get anywhere with the flower."

He nodded, but his gaze looked doubtful. I was a little doubtful, too. But I'd never seen a flower like that. Surely it couldn't grow in too many places in London.

# 15

*Eve*

Lachlan and I parted ways without another word, and I strode through the cemetery, passing my mother's headstone with a twinge to my heart. I told myself I'd visit soon, using an invisibility potion. It was a good compromise.

When I reached the main courtyard, I avoided the coffee shop that had so enticed me and headed for the main part of town. I could grab one somewhere out of shifter territory.

As I walked, I pulled out my mobile and sent a quick text to Seraphia. As both a goddess of plants and a librarian, she was the perfect person to ask. She spent most nights in the Underworld at her mate's castle.

Hades would probably never adjust to living out in Guild City, but there was a portal connecting his realm to her library, so she commuted.

A few moments later, her return text informed me that she could open up early.

Thank fates.

I hurried through the streets, enjoying the quiet. I loved this town more than any place on earth, and the early morning hours were some of my favorites. The streets smelled of coffee and fresh bread as the bakeries and shops got up and running. I stopped in one of my favorites to get a chocolate pastry and a coffee, then kept moving, finally reaching Seraphia's library. It was a small building, constructed of the dark timber frames and white plaster that were traditional on Tudor structures. The ancient diamond-pane windows revealed little of the interior.

I tried the handle, finding it still locked, but Seraphia appeared a few seconds later and opened the door. Her hair was messy and her makeup undone, and gratitude welled within me. "Thank you so much for showing up early," I said.

"No problem." She smiled and motioned me inside. "Come on."

I entered the library, which was actually a massive space squeezed into Guild City with magic. The mixed scent of wood, paper, and leather welcomed me, and I breathed deeply. My footsteps echoed on the floor, and the place held the kind of holy silence that character-ized the best libraries. The main atrium had a massive soaring dome for a ceiling, and hundreds of tall wooden bookshelves spread out from there.

"Do you have some paper and a pen?" I asked.

"Sure thing." She drew me over to a small sitting room by the door. The space was cozy, with a fire blazing merrily in the hearth and a little desk in front of the window. I sat at the desk and took the pencil and paper she handed me, then got to work.

"I'm just going to get a coffee," she said. "Do you want one?"

"Please." I could definitely use another. And prob-ably a third.

I worked quickly, trying to remember every detail of the flower. It wasn't easy, but fortunately, I wasn't a terrible artist. By the time Seraphia returned, I had a good enough picture. She handed me the coffee, and I showed her the paper, which she studied, frowning. "You're no Darwin, but this isn't bad. Where did you find the flower?"

"In the trouser cuff of the killer. Stuck there like he'd walked through a garden."

"It's a Helleborensius, a magical version of the Helle-bore plant. They're very rare."

"That's what I hoped. Do you know of anywhere they grow in London?"

"No, but I can try to find out." Excitement glinted in

her eyes. Seraphia loved a mystery just as much as I did. "Come on."

I followed her back to the atrium, where the domed ceiling soared overhead. She waved a hand, and a massive fire flared to life, right in the middle of the tile floor.

The card catalog at Seraphia's library was just a *little* different than other ones.

"Could you hold this?" She shoved her coffee into my hands without waiting for a response, then pulled a notepad from her pocket, along with a tiny stub of pencil. Quickly, she wrote a message on the paper, then tore it off and chucked it into the flames. She took her coffee back and sipped. "Shouldn't be but a moment."

I watched, my breath held, as smoke curled up from the fire in a slender spiral. It drifted back into the stacks, creating a faint ribbon for us to follow.

"Come on." Seraphia started after the smoke, and I followed.

"What did you ask it for?"

"Any book that contained a mention of Helleborensius in London."

I crossed my fingers that we would find it in our city.

The smoke led us around the library, pointing out book after book, and even a few rolled-up maps stored on a massive case at the back. When we'd collected our loot, Seraphia found us a table.

Together, we searched. And searched. And searched.

It was after noon by the time we finished, and my eyes burned from trying to read the tiny text. But my heart was light.

Seraphia grinned at me. "Well, that was productive."

"Just one place in London." I grinned. "Who would have thought?"

"With any luck, he lives there."

The flower could only be found in Richmond Park, the largest Royal Park in London. It even had deer. The perfect place for a shifter to hide out.

I prayed he actually lived there. Even if Lachlan got the name of a recently released criminal that his father had put away, that still wouldn't necessarily tell us where the bastard was hiding.

"Thank you, Seraphia. I can't tell you how much this helps," I said.

She reached across the table and gripped my hand. "Of course. Anything." She frowned. "Are you sure you're all right? You've seemed off lately."

"Off?" I gave my voice a confused note, but I knew exactly what she was talking about. I felt like a fish out of water, a boat on dry land, a city after an earthquake. Things were *so* not right in my world.

"Yeah," she said. "Just, a little different. Stressed."

"I'm wanted for murder."

"Yeah. And that's a big deal, don't get me wrong. But..."

I swallowed hard, the words wanting to escape: *I've*

*been lying about my species the whole time.* It wasn't the worst lie. I *knew* that. My friends were true friends. They'd understand my reasoning. It didn't matter to them what I was.

"I'll tell you when this is all over, all right?" And I meant it. The promise lifted a weight off my shoulders, and I grinned.

"All right. Just be careful, okay? Let us know if you need any more help."

"Will do. And thanks again." I left quickly, taking the tiny map of Richmond Park that we'd found. It had been made by the Royal Botanic Society about thirty years ago and showed the locations of many of the flower beds in the park. Things could have changed since then, but it was a start.

The fact that the killer was living out in human London was definitely a problem, especially if he was mad. I just prayed he still had enough sense left to keep his species a secret.

*Lachlan*

Glencarrough wasn't far from our ancestral lands in the Highlands. They adjoined each other at their northern and southern sides, making it easy to reach them.

Fortunately, the Alpha at Glencarrough, a regal woman named Eleanor, had agreed to meet me on our turf. I needed to see the seer again, and we were running out of time.

I waited for her by the stone circle and was grateful when she appeared on time, wearing a dark cloak that blew in the wind with her graying hair pulled up around her face. The steel in her eyes reminded me of my father. No doubt it would remind others of me.

"Eleanor. Thank you for meeting me."

She nodded, her gaze somber. "There are terrible things happening in Guild City, from what I hear."

"Two murders. My father's grave desecrated."

Sadness flashed in her eyes. "Your poor father. How are you?"

"Fine."

"Fine? Hardly." She looked me up and down. "You look like you could use a week on a beach."

"When does an Alpha ever get a week on the beach?"

She laughed softly. "Don't try to distract me. This can't be easy for you."

"It's fine." She didn't know I took the potion to suppress any errant emotions. Had no idea that I feared the Dark Moon curse, in fact. "Were you able to find the names of anyone that my father put away for a particularly long time while he was with the security force?"

"Aye. I served with him, which you might not have known."

"I didn't."

"Well, he was good at his job. There are three individuals that have been released after doing their time, though I'm not sure that any of them would have done this."

"Do you know where they are?"

"I do not. They left our land, understandably so. But their names were Finn MacCallum, Douglas Connor, and Sean Faraday."

"Thank you."

She nodded. "I'll see if I can find anything else about them, and if I do, I'll let you know."

We said our goodbyes, and she departed.

For the second time in as many days, I entered the stone circle and made the blood sacrifice required. Now that I had the three names, perhaps the seer could help more.

After a few moments, her cottage appeared, and I approached. I reached her door and knocked, waiting only a few seconds for her to open it.

Her eyes widened. "More questions?"

I nodded. "Aye. May I come in?"

"You're lucky I answered a second time." She shook her head, sorrow in her eyes. "But I can sense the tragedy that is happening in Guild City."

She stepped back and gestured for me to enter. I

breathed shallowly, hating the thickly perfumed air. She shut the door and followed me deeper into her suite. "What is it?"

I gave her the three names. "What can you tell me about them?"

"You want to know if they're your murderer."

"I do."

She frowned. "You know I probably can't see that. Not without them being here."

"What can you tell me? Anything will be helpful."

She shrugged. "Let's see, shall we?"

Gracefully, she strode to a small pink couch and sat. I waited, uncomfortable and impatient, as she closed her eyes and began to hum low in her throat.

Her magic swelled on the air, the faint scent of powder and rose blossoms. Minutes passed, until finally, she opened her eyes. "One of them is dead. Just recently. Finn MacCallum has left this plane. The other two are alive, and not far from here. Both in the UK. Douglas Connor may even be in London."

I nodded. "Good. Thank you. Can you tell me where?"

"No, not specifically. But I'm certain he's there." She frowned. "He's been there a month. Perhaps a little more, but not much."

I'd take what I could get. This was further than we'd been.

"Will there be anything else?" she asked.

The question popped out of my lips before I could stop it. "The girl who was meant to be my mate. Where is she?"

Her eyes flared wide. "You've never asked this before."

Guilt stabbed me. Duty had kept me moving...but *she* had been my duty. Taking her as my mate had been foretold by fate itself. And yet, I'd ignored it.

I'd *had* to.

From the moment I'd met her—that brief flash of time—I'd known she'd be the death of me. She had the ability to make me feel so deeply that I'd fall to the Dark Moon curse.

It had been a calculated sacrifice. No matter what fate wanted from me, I had to ignore her to protect my clan. They couldn't lose another Alpha to the curse.

But now that I was starting to feel something for another, I needed to know what had happened to her.

"I know I haven't asked this before," I said. "And I had good reason. But I need to know now."

"She is your destiny, and yet, you have avoided it. I understand why. You don't want to fall to the curse the way your father did. And it was wise of you to be concerned."

Hearing her say it made ice stab me in the chest. She confirmed that the Dark Moon curse stalked me.

"I need to know," I said. "Can you find her?"

"I can already tell you no. She disappeared from my sight eight years ago."

"Dead?" The icicle in my heart twisted. That was two years after she'd disappeared from Guild City.

"I don't know. Perhaps."

"What else could it be?"

She shook her head. "I have no idea. But she is lost to me."

I clenched my fist, disappointed. "Thank you for your help."

I left, returning to Guild City.

Douglas Connor. He could be our killer. He could even be in London.

After I arrived in Guild City, I ran into Eve in the courtyard outside my guild tower. Her eyes were bright, and her silvery pink hair gleamed under the sun.

I stared, entranced by her. The sight of her felt more welcome than a hot shower after a fight. More welcome than my bed after a long day. Impossible thoughts ran through my mind.

Finally, I asked, "Did you find something?"

"I did." She grinned widely. "Richmond Park."

"The big one in London?"

"The very same. This flower only grows there. At least, in London. It's a rare variety."

"Let's go. Immediately." I was going to find that bastard Douglas. "I don't have a transport charm, but it shouldn't take long to get there." I strode past her, headed for one of the city gates.

"Excellent." She hurried to join me. "What did you find?"

"Two names, still living. Both men. One in London. Douglas Connor."

"Douglas Connor. Our murderer?"

"Perhaps."

She nodded. "Let's go find him. The gate through the Haunted Hound is closest."

We hurried through town, getting several looks as we passed through the main city street. I was rarely seen with a woman, and Eve was more than just any woman.

We reached the massive gate that led out of town and took the portal to the Haunted Hound. I rarely visited human London, preferring Scotland if I were going to leave Guild City.

But Eve apparently came here often. As we passed through the main part of the pub, the man behind the bar grinned widely at the sight of her.

Quinn McKay.

The only shifter in town who had left our pack but still lived in Guild City. It was an odd arrangement, but when the Shadow Guild had appeared, it had called to him. I nodded at him. I knew other Alphas who might be territorial about a nearby shifter not belonging to the pack, but I only wanted the willing.

The girl who'd run from me had certainly been unwilling.

"Eve." Quinn smiled at her and leaned over the bar. "What can I do for you?"

"Just passing through, Quinn."

Quinn's grin widened. "Passing through my heart."

It was a ridiculous line, and most probably a joke between the two of them. Still, the jealousy rose. My wolf went wild with it, rising inside me like a beast, scrabbling to get out. I forced it back, but not before I heard a faint growl come from my throat.

*Fuck.*

What the hell was I doing?

Apparently, Eve and Quinn had heard as well, because they both turned to me, eyes wide.

I patted my chest. "Something caught in my throat."

Quinn gave me a knowing look, and I stared him down. After a few seconds, he diverted his gaze, forced by the chain of dominance.

"Let's go." Eve gestured me forward. "Thanks, Quinn, I'll see you later."

I followed Eve out into London proper, ignoring Quinn's stare. With shaking hands, I withdrew the flask from my pocket and took several deep gulps, praying that the stronger potion would work.

What the hell was happening to me?

## 16

*Eve*

My head spun as I hurried out into London. Lachlan had just *growled* at Quinn for flirting with me.

*Growled.*

Even his eyes had gone bright green. His wolf could sense that I was his mate, even though his human mind hadn't caught up. That potion that he drank was helping, for sure. Thank fates he was hooked on it.

But even as I thought it, I felt guilty as hell. It would be terrible to live without emotion. Even more terrible to fight every day to suppress it so that you could do your duty by your people.

I shook the thoughts away. There was no time for

sympathy for Lachlan. I needed to keep my head in the game.

The Haunted Hound was located in Covent Garden, a charming part of London full of pubs and shops. Richmond Park was clear across town, however, so I flagged a black cab that went rumbling past.

"This good with you?" I asked as it rolled to a stop.

"It's fine."

We climbed in together, and I made a point to sit as far from him as possible.

The cabbie leaned back over the seat. He was an older man with a shock of white hair and dark eyes. "Where will it be?"

"Richmond Park," Lachlan said.

"Have you there in the blink of an eye."

We rode in silence. Fortunately, traffic was light, and the cabbie drove like a demon. By the time we arrived, my head was spinning from the speed at which he'd taken the turns.

Lachlan paid, and we climbed out. The park itself was massive, a rambling garden with thousands of acres of wild green space.

"Do you know roughly where these flowers are?" he asked.

I pulled the little map from my pocket. "It says here that they should be at the back, in a bed planted by Queen Victoria."

"Lead the way."

The park was quiet as we cut through. There were a few people picnicking and sunbathing at the front, but as we reached the more wooded area, it turned empty. The air prickled with an eerie chill, and I looked at Lachlan. "Magic."

He nodded. "He's trying to keep people away, and it's working."

"He's got some connections if he can manage that."

Generally speaking, shifters didn't do that kind of magic. He'd have to be connected to a sorceress or witch of some kind to get a spell like that.

The shadows in the park grew darker as we moved deeper. We were nearly to the end when Lachlan stiffened. "Do you smell that?"

"No." I sniffed, then caught the faintest scent of copper. My heart rocketed into my throat. "Blood?"

"Not human."

It was too much to hope that it was our murderer.

"This way." Lachlan turned left and cut through the trees, moving swiftly and silently.

I followed, albeit not as quietly. I was no slouch, but I didn't quite have his talent.

We came across the deer a few moments later. The creature had been torn to pieces. As soon as I laid eyes on it, I looked away, up into the trees. "How long ago?" I asked.

There was silence for a moment, before Lachlan answered. "Less than twenty-four hours, I'd guess."

"Was it him?"

"It was a wolf or another large predator. So it was probably our man."

"He's living back here and eating the deer."

"Only a feral wolf would do that."

"Dark Moon curse." I shivered. Would I ever fall prey to it?

*Please, God, no.*

Lachlan pulled out his mobile, and I heard him make a call for a cleanup team to take care of the remains. The last thing we needed was humans suspecting that a massive wild animal was loose in the park. They did *not* need to find our guy before we did. Not only was he a threat to Lachlan's wolves, but he could reveal our secret to the humans.

"Let's keep moving." Lachlan pressed on, and I followed, widely skirting the carnage.

I consulted the map once more, then led us through the park toward the flowers. It took a few tries to find it, but finally, we found a small patch of the Helleborensius.

"This is it." I knelt and touched them.

"I'm going to shift. My senses are better in that form."

I nodded, averting my gaze. It wasn't like I could see anything when he shifted—the cloud of green magic obscured him—but somehow, it felt intimate.

*Way* too intimate with Lachlan.

Magic sparked on the air, and a moment later, I looked back and saw the massive wolf. He was truly gorgeous. Absolutely huge, far bigger than any other wolf I'd ever seen, with jet-black fur and brilliant eyes. He looked at me for one long moment, and I shivered.

It was almost as if he could see into my soul in that form. What else could he sense?

"Well?" I asked. "Smell anything?"

He turned around and prowled through the garden, his strides long and powerful. Just watching him gave me a thrill and made me wish that I could transform as well.

After a while, he shifted back. "There's nothing out of the ordinary here," he said. "There was a rain recently, and it's covered up the scent of anyone who walked through."

"Let's keep looking, then. There's still quite a bit of park around here."

We set off, moving silently through the woods. Now that we'd reached the killer's turf, tension tightened my shoulders. I reached into the ether and withdrew my bag, then pulled a potion bomb free before stowing my bag away. As Lachlan arched a brow, I shrugged. "I like to be prepared."

He nodded. "You're skilled at that."

"Very."

I crept forward, my gaze alert on the forest around

us. The air began to prickle sharply, increasing in intensity until tears sprung to my eyes. "You feel that?"

"A powerful repelling charm."

It looked like there was just forest ahead of us, but there had to be more. There was no way a charm like this would be here unless someone was trying to hide something.

"Wait here," Lachlan said. "I can try to break through."

"No, the pain would drive you mad. I've felt this kind of curse before. Made it myself. It's horrible."

"It's done with potions?"

"It is. Sprinkled on the ground. You need a witch to finish it, though."

"So he's got a witch and a potion master on his side."

"Could just be one very talented witch." I raised my wrist and looked at the leather band studded with vials of potion. "I have something that will help us get through. It's just one dose, so we'll have to share."

"It won't work as well then, I assume."

"It'll be fine. Better than you trying to go alone."

"You take it, and I'll push on."

I glared at him. "You can't make it through without some protection. I'm serious when I say it will drive you mad. And you can't afford that."

His gaze turned dark, and he knew what I meant. The Dark Moon curse.

I didn't know if this kind of protection charm carried

that risk, but it really would hurt so badly that he'd go crazy from the pain. No need to tempt fate, especially if his goal was to save me a bit of pain. I could take it.

Quickly, I removed the vial from my wrist cuff and opened it, then swigged back half and passed it over to him. Cold magic raced down my limbs as he drank the other half, staring at me the whole while.

I looked away, staring through the invisible barrier.

Once he'd finished his potion, I stepped forward.

Immediately, the pain made me wince. It felt like tiny daggers stabbing me all over. My breath grew short, and tears sprang to my eyes again. I pushed onward, every inch of me in agony until it was too much. I couldn't go any farther.

But I couldn't step backward, either.

I was stuck, my muscles turned to jelly with pain.

Heat surrounded me, and Lachlan swept me into his arms, lunging through the last of the barrier. The pain disappeared immediately, and I gasped, trying to catch my breath.

"Are you all right?" Concern gleamed in his eyes as he looked down at me.

"Yeah." I pushed weakly at his chest, and he let me down.

We turned to face the clearing, immediately spotting a little cottage underneath a huge tree. It looked ancient, made of stone and thatch. There was no glass in the windows, and weeds grew around the base.

"Whoa." I jerked, surprised. I hadn't seen it at all when we'd been on the other side of the barrier. Was he in there?

"It's empty," Lachlan said. "I can feel it."

Damn it.

But part of me was grateful, too. The brief moment that Lachlan had spent holding me could have turned deadly if the killer had been in the cabin, watching.

Lachlan strode forward, and I followed, my footsteps silent on the grass.

The killer lived here. He had to. There was no other reason for it to be protected like this.

Unless it was the home of the witch who'd helped him.

But wouldn't we know if a powerful witch lived outside Guild City? There were plenty of supernaturals living among the humans in London, and most people in Guild City knew of the most powerful ones, the same way humans knew about movie stars.

"Do you smell that?" Lachlan asked.

"Not another dead body..." The scent hit me then— the powerful stench of rotten eggs. "Sulfur?"

"Likely meant to hide his scent so that no one will recognize him." Lachlan sounded disgusted. "It wouldn't even help if I shifted. It overpowers everything."

"He expected that we might find him."

"He was playing it safe, at least."

Damn. I stopped in front of the cottage door alongside Lachlan. We both held our hands over the door, testing to see if we felt any dangerous magic.

"Seems like we made it through the worst of it." Carefully, he gripped the doorknob and turned.

No lock.

It creaked as its swung open, revealing the dark interior of a shabby little cottage.

"Ew." It was a disgusting mess. Like an animal had lived there.

"He probably stays in his wolf form much of the time."

"Then why sleep in the cottage?"

Lachlan frowned. "Maybe he doesn't have connections like we thought. Maybe he stumbled on this place and was so mad already that it didn't matter if he crossed the protective barrier."

I stepped inside, prickling with awareness. There were booze bottles scattered around, along with old clothes and a dirty straw mattress. The fireplace was devoid of wood, and it looked like a family of rodents had set up house in all of the four corners of the cottage.

Lachlan pulled out his mobile and made a quick call for backup. "When we're done here," he explained to me, "they'll guard the place. Our man might not come back, but I want someone waiting for him if he does."

I nodded, continuing my search. Every minute I spent in there made my skin grow colder and my bones feel more brittle. The very walls felt like they were steeped in his madness.

"Under here." Lachlan knelt by the mattress and held it up.

Beneath it lay a dagger stained red with blood.

"Holy fates," I breathed.

"He used it to kill Bill." A grim frown slashed across his face.

"I can track him with that. Maybe."

He looked at me. "Really?"

I nodded. "That's a powerful object. He used it to murder someone. It has enough residual energy that I should be able to make a potion that will turn it into a tracking device."

"It would find him anywhere?"

"As long as he's not on the other side of the world, yes."

He nodded. "Good. That's good."

"Understatement much?"

The corner of his mouth pulled up at the side, one of the very rare smiles I'd ever seen him give.

"Can we touch it?" he asked.

"Maybe not with our bare skin. I don't want to dilute the energy."

Lachlan looked around, no doubt searching for a clean enough cloth that we could wrap it in.

There was nothing, of course. Everything in the place was utterly filthy with dust and grime.

He removed his leather jacket and laid it aside, then stripped off the shirt underneath. I looked away quickly, but not before I got a glimpse of smooth skin and a broad chest.

"Here." He handed me the shirt, and I took it without looking at him.

The shirt was still warm from his skin, and it felt like it burned into me. As I carefully gathered up the knife and stored it in my bag in the ether, he put his jacket back on and zipped it up.

"All right. Let's get out of here." I stood.

We made our way back through the park, reaching Guild City less than an hour later. It was dusk, and the streetlamps were beginning to go on. Shop windows glowed golden and bright.

He escorted me back to the Shadow Guild tower, ignoring me when I told him not to bother. The quickest route was via a narrow alley that led straight to our courtyard, and I led the way.

As soon as I stepped into the courtyard, a strong hand gripped my arm and yanked me to the side.

I screamed, lashing out as pain flared. Everything happened in a blur.

My attacker yanked me to him, his arm tight around my throat. I struck out with my elbow, nailing him in the gut. He just grunted, and I tried to stamp on his foot as I scrabbled to get one of the potions in my leather cuff.

A growl sounded, and a dark figure lunged, leaping high, right toward us.

The bastard hurled me against the wall so hard that my head crashed against it. My vision went fuzzy as I slid to the ground.

I was barely able to see Lachlan, in wolf form, drag the hooded man away from me. They grappled until his brilliant wolf's eyes caught me lying on the ground. He released the man, who scrambled away and sprinted down the alley.

Lachlan let him go, returning to his human form and racing to me. Gently, he lifted me up, cradling me against his chest. "Eve, wake up, Eve." Fear echoed in his voice.

"Lachlan." My voice sounded scratchy, and my head ached.

The fear in his eyes was stark, worry creasing his face as he gently touched my head. "You're bleeding. Do you have a healing potion?"

Weakly, I raised my wrist. "Pink one."

He pulled the tiny vial free and held it to my lips. As I drank, the pain began to fade. I could feel my wound knitting itself back together.

I met his gaze, still shadowed with concern. "You let him go."

"The blood around your head. I thought you might be—"

He didn't say it, but I knew what he'd thought.

"You thought I might be dying." So he'd let the killer go.

How had it all happened so fast?

He nodded, staring down at me.

"Did you see him?" I asked.

"No. Not his face."

Full darkness had fallen, and I could feel the silent emptiness of the tower behind us. The Shadow Guild was so small and new that our courtyard was entirely empty. The row of shops across the way was abandoned, not a single one open.

The resulting stillness to the air created a bubble around us. We could have been the only ones in the world, and it was the strangest sensation to be cocooned in the darkness with him.

The way he looked at me...

It made my breath catch in my throat. The heat in his eyes was combined with confusion. Fear.

"Eve." He pulled me to him, as if unable to help himself.

I could stop him. I had a few seconds to push him away. To say no.

But somehow, I'd lost my mind.

Something in me pulled toward him, so hard that it was impossible to resist. In that moment, I had to kiss him.

I wrapped my arms around his neck and pressed my lips to his.

Sparks flashed between us, bright and brilliant, as desire streaked through me, lighting up my nerve endings.

He groaned low in his throat, his lips parting so that he could kiss me more deeply. His strong arms held me against his broad chest, and he kissed me like it had been years since he'd touched another.

Maybe it had.

All of the pent-up frustration and desire that had been ricocheting back and forth between us exploded. I could kiss him forever.

When he pulled away, I suddenly felt cold. Alone.

Shocked, I looked up at him. Heat still glinted in his eyes, and his breath came heavy with desire.

"Eve." His voice was rough but firm. "Tell me what's going on with you. Tell me why I feel this way."

"I don't know what you mean."

"I have a mate. *Had* a mate." He dragged a hand through his hair. "I feel like I'm losing my mind. And maybe I am. But you must be her. I can feel it in my soul."

Ice chilled my bones, and I pulled away from him. "I have no idea what you're talking about."

"This is your chance to come clean," he said, his voice desperate. "Explain how you're doing this."

I stood upright, backing against the wall. He stood as well, chest heaving.

"You must be losing it," I said. "Because I don't know what you're talking about."

His gaze shuttered, and I saw something unidentifiable in his eyes.

*You must be losing it.*

I could hear what I'd just said, played over and over in my mind. He had only one fear in the entire world—falling to the Dark Moon curse. I'd just accused him of being crazy. And he *wasn't*. He was figuring it out, just as I'd feared he would.

But I was gaslighting him.

I was a dick.

Anger clouded his eyes.

Before he could say anything, four figures appeared behind him: Carrow, Seraphia, Mac, and Beatrix.

My friends.

Desperate, I stepped away from the wall and darted around him. It was the coward's way out, but I took it. I probably should have come clean, but I couldn't. I just couldn't. For both of our sakes. He had the potion to keep himself sane. He didn't need me confirming that I was his mate, not when that bond would be the death of us. Of me, at the very least.

"Is everything okay here?" Carrow's expression turned dark as she looked Lachlan up and down.

"No." Lachlan's voice was firm. "Someone just attacked Eve. She can't be left alone."

"I need to go make the potion to track him," I said,

ignoring his words and the shocked gazes of my friends. I just had to get away from him.

*Now.*

I strode toward the tower, but he followed. "I'm not letting you out of my sight. Not while he's out there."

Carrow and the rest of my friends shoved their way in between him and me. He glowered but stepped back.

"We can protect her," Carrow said.

They could, too. They had some pretty incredible magic.

Lachlan frowned, seeming to accept that he wasn't getting inside the tower. "Fine. I'll stand guard out here until my men arrive. There will be a guard on this tower twenty-four-seven."

"Suit yourself," Carrow said. "They just can't come in."

I didn't look at him as I hurried into the tower. From the way his gaze burned into me, this wasn't going to be the last of it.

**17**

---

*Eve*

My body buzzed as I walked into the main room of the Shadow Guild tower. I reached the middle of the large room before I had to stop and suck in a deep breath.

"Everything all right?" Carrow asked.

"Is he still out there?" I turned to find my four friends staring at me.

Seraphia went to peek out the window. "Yes." She looked back at me. "And he's staring at this place like there's treasure inside. Treasure that he doesn't really like."

I grimaced.

She leaned against the window and gave me a sympathetic smile and a thumbs-up. The gesture of support lit a little fire of warmth in my chest. Now was the time to confess, and she knew it. I'd promised her the truth, and there was no better time.

"I'll be right back," said Mac, then raced up the stairs and returned in twenty seconds flat with a chocolate bar. "You looked like you could use this."

"You're a genius."

"I'm going to get the wine," Carrow said.

"I don't have time for a drink."

"I do." She gave me a long look. "And you might find you want a little sip."

"Yeah." I shoved the chocolate bar in my mouth as she waited, chewing with the fervor of an accountant crunching numbers on tax day.

She was back with the wine in a flash, and I nodded toward the floor above. "I've got to make this potion, but I need to tell you guys something."

"I figured." Carrow gripped the wine bottle and headed up the stairs.

I followed, feeling the words start to spill out as soon as I reached my workshop. I'd intended to get started on the potion while I spoke, but once they began flowing, I couldn't do anything else except tell the whole damned story.

As I talked, Carrow passed around the wine. I took a small glass and gulped the whole thing, then put it aside. I couldn't afford another if I was going to keep my wits about me.

When I neared the end of my story, I held up the pendant around my neck. "And this is what keeps my true species hidden." Finally, I trailed off. "So, that's that. I've been lying this whole time."

Carrow hopped up onto one of my worktables and swigged her wine. "Sure have. But...whatever."

Mac nodded. "Sounds like you had good reasons."

Seraphia and Beatrix nodded their agreement.

Relief flushed through me.

"You didn't expect us to be mad, did you?" Carrow asked.

"Not really. You guys are too great not to understand. But I still feel like shit." I walked toward the window and looked down at Lachlan, who stared up at my window. His gaze snagged on me, anger flashing in his eyes' depths. I ducked back behind the wall. "I'm pretty sure he thinks I *am* shit."

"He wouldn't think that," Carrow said. "I mean, he'd be pissed as hell and maybe not forgive you—"

Mac hissed at her, clearly not liking that.

"What?" Carrow said. "It's fine if he doesn't forgive her. She doesn't want to be with him, anyway."

"She's right. I don't." I grimaced. "I mean, I don't know. It's not like I'm imagining some future where I ride off into the sunset with him. But I do feel horrible for what I said to him."

Mac shook her head. "It was a dick move, yes. But the seer was very clear that going down the fated mate path would lead to your death. It was the only reasonable thing you could have done."

The rest of my friends nodded their agreement.

"Lies suck," Carrow said. "But you had decent reasons." She frowned. "I will say that prophecies don't always turn out how you expect, though."

"I hope you're right about that." I smiled. "Thanks, guys."

"Now, how can we help with this potion?" Seraphia rubbed her hands together.

The other three nodded, and gratitude welled within me. "You're the best."

I pointed out ingredients and set them to chopping and measuring. On the other side of the room, I got the little cauldron heating and began to add everything into the pot, measuring twice to make sure it was all correct.

I couldn't help but think of Lachlan as I worked, but none of my thoughts made sense. They were endless circles of confusion and desire and regret. Everything was a mess between us, and the only thing I was certain of was that it couldn't be fixed.

Finally, the potion was nearly done. As the final ingredient was stirred in, my friends joined me, watching.

"It should only be a few more minutes," I said. "Can someone go check the courtyard?" The idea of him being out there still made me twitchy.

Beatrix went to the window. "He's gone, but there are

two dozen shifters out there, and they're all dressed in the security uniform."

Mac joined and whistled low. "That's quite the crowd."

*He wants to protect me.*

The thought started to soften me, but I shoved it away. For our sakes, I couldn't go down that path, especially since the person he had to protect me from was himself.

When the cauldron stopped smoking, I drew my bag from the ether and removed the cloth-wrapped dagger. I could feel the avid gazes of my friends as I unwrapped the bloodstained weapon. Just touching it made my stomach turn. Quickly, I dipped the blade in the cauldron, grateful when the red blood was replaced by the gleaming purple potion. I could feel the magic vibrating up through the hilt. "It's done."

"We need to take it to Lachlan," Carrow said.

I frowned.

She held up her hands. "No arguments. I know you don't want to see him, but we're not hunting this murderer ourselves. It's shifter business."

She was right. He deserved to know. It had been a passing, cowardly fancy of mine to finish the job on my own.

Anyway, the killer was strong. I wouldn't risk my friends for this. Not when Lachlan wanted to handle it himself.

"I'll take it to him." I wrapped it back up in the cloth and put in the bag, which I returned to the ether.

"We'll come with," Mac said.

"Thank you."

"Duh." She grinned.

Together, we left the tower and headed down into our formerly quiet courtyard. Twenty-four pairs of eyes stared at me, and I smiled weakly.

I looked for the leader, planning to tell them where we were headed, but they all looked of equal rank. Didn't matter. They didn't have any say over me.

My friends and I pushed our way through the crowd, the shifters parting reluctantly to let us pass. They followed us single file down the narrow alley and out into the main part of Guild City, then all the way down the High Street to the shifters' tower.

Lachlan came out to the main steps to meet us, no doubt having already heard about the mass of shifters making their way through town.

"It's done," I said, unable to make eye contact. I knew I should try to further prove I wasn't a shifter, but I just couldn't bear to look at him.

"Come inside." His voice was stiff. "Do you need anything to make the spell work?"

"A map."

He nodded and turned around, heading back in. I could almost feel the anger he left in his wake, and I looked at my friends. They all gave me identical forced smiles, their eyes too bright. *Everyone* could feel how awkward this was.

"You guys look crazy," I whispered.

"This feels crazy," Mac whispered.

"True story." I turned back to follow Lachlan, and my friends joined us.

The main room was only about half full, but the occupants cleared out when they saw Lachlan. A few moments later, Kenneth appeared, a collection of rolled-up maps clutched in his hands.

"Thank you." Lachlan took the maps and spread them out.

"Let's start with one of London," I said. "Surely he didn't stay in Guild City. It's too dangerous."

Lachlan nodded and unrolled a map. My friends crowded around, along with the same twenty-four guards who'd been standing in my courtyard.

Carefully, I removed the dagger from the bag and unwrapped it. I held the very end of the hilt gently and dangled the dagger over the map. The blade began to spin in a circle, seeking our target.

It finally stopped moving, right over Guild City.

"Still here." Lachlan unrolled another map and laid it out.

The familiar streets of Guild City appeared, and I held my breath as I dangled the blade over the map. It spun in circles for a few moments, the entire group watching with anticipation.

Finally, it stopped.

Right on the Shifter Guild's tower.

"He's here," I whispered, fear shivering over my skin.

Lachlan's head shot up, his gaze meeting mine. "Could this be wrong?"

"No. It can't be." It pointed right at the tower. Not at a specific room because of the way the map was drawn, but it was clear he was somewhere within these walls.

"Do you have a plan of the tower?" I asked.

"No. The building's never had one that I know of. We'll have to search it ourselves." Lachlan turned to his guards. "Clear the tower of all civilians. Get them into the city center, and use as many forces as you need. The rest will stay here to help us look." He turned to me. "You need to leave now. It's too dangerous."

"No." I shook my head. "No way in hell. I want to help catch this guy."

I knew I *should* go. It was the safest thing. Cut out now. My job was done, right? I'd cleared my name.

But as much as I stood by my secrets, I felt a little guilty about all the lies. They'd been necessary, but I hated what I'd said to Lachlan. I wasn't going to bail now. "I'm going to help you find him, and it will take you more time to fight me on that than you can afford."

His jaw tightened, but I could see it in his eyes when he realized I was right.

I looked at my friends. "You guys should get out of here, though."

Carrow laughed in my face, Mac joining her. Seraphia and Beatrix just looked at me like I'd grown two heads.

"We've got your back, dummy," Mac said. "And it will take you longer to fight *us* on that than you can afford."

Despite my terror, a low laugh escaped me. "Oh, you bitch, using my own words against me."

She hugged me quickly, then pulled back. "Come on, let's go find a murderer."

After Lachlan's troops scattered, he turned to the five of us. "My men are spreading out. We're going as a group."

He probably had some chivalrous idea about protecting us in his head. And truth was, I appreciated it. I didn't think it was entirely necessary, but I still remembered the grip of the killer's arm around my neck. So I wasn't going to argue. I wanted my friends safe, and grouping up would help ensure that.

Carrow frowned. "We can split up into two groups. It'd be faster, and we'll be okay."

I nodded, fine with it. As much as I wanted to wrap them all in cotton wool, it wasn't my call. Carrow was the leader of our group, and she was right. Besides, Seraphia was a damned goddess, and Carrow was so powerful, it made my eyes cross sometimes. Mac and Beatrix were no slouches, either.

Lachlan was wise enough not to argue until Carrow gestured for Beatrix and me to join her. He growled low, then grimaced. This time, he didn't even try to pretend that it was something caught in his throat.

Carrow looked at me, and I shrugged. "It's fine, I'll go with him."

"All right." She nodded. "Mac's with me, then."

Mac nodded and joined her. I couldn't help but notice that Carrow had put the goddess with me, as if she knew I were at greater risk.

I rubbed my throat, still feeling the grip of the killer. Maybe I was.

Didn't matter. We were going to catch this bastard and end this.

"We'll take the third floor, if you want the fourth," Lachlan said to her. "You'll see my security team as you search. There will be about twenty of them combing the tower."

Carrow nodded and took off, her team behind her.

"This way." Lachlan turned and headed to another set of stairs.

Seraphia caught my eye. "You okay?"

I nodded. "I'm a big girl."

She grinned. "Then let's go."

I might have been a big girl, but I decided to let her take the middle of our little pack. Being too close to Lachlan distracted me, and I needed all the focus I could get.

As we climbed up the stairs, I removed a stunner from my bag in the ether. The potion bomb was a comforting weight in my hand as I climbed. I offered one to Seraphia, but she shook her head, raising her hands to show two tiny vines resting in her palms. In the blink of an eye, she could make them big enough to strangle a man.

We reached the third floor and moved silently down the hall, checking the various rooms and closets. Every now and again, I heard the little charm at Lachlan's wrist emit a tiny voice announcing various cleared spaces.

Together, we searched room after room. Bedrooms, sitting rooms, kitchens, meeting rooms, every kind of room one could imagine—and they were all empty. I kept thinking that I saw a shadow out of the corner of my eye, but whenever I turned, it was gone. The feeling kept getting stronger and stronger, until my hair was on end.

When the attack came, it happened so fast that I couldn't even scream. One second, I was looking at Seraphia's back, and the next, a hand was around my mouth, yanking me toward the wall.

Only there was no wall anymore.

A doorway had appeared.

*It hadn't been there before.*

Panic tore my mind in two as the killer yanked me into the secret passage and the door disappeared. Everything went black as I heard the sound of Lachlan's shout.

Frantic, I slammed my potion bomb toward the body that held me in an iron grip. Quick as a snake, he slapped it out of my hand.

It shattered uselessly against the ground.

I thrashed, trying to break his hold, but he just tightened it.

"Calm the fuck down," he growled, his voice barely human. It sounded almost like he was about to shift.

*Totally feral.*

Oh, fates. What would happen if he did shift? Would he lose his mind entirely and tear me apart?

I had to be clever. How to play this? No one was coming. If they could have found the entrance to this secret passage, they'd be here by now.

I stopped fighting for the most part, needing to get to my leather cuff. There were potions there that could help me. As he dragged me down the hall, I reached for one, my hands trembling.

"What are you doing?" he growled, clearly sensing that something was up.

I made a muffled noise, trying to sound panicked. It wasn't hard.

Instead of responding, he knocked my head against the wall so hard that pain exploded like fireworks behind my eyes. A half second later, everything faded away.

## 18

*Eve*

I woke with the worst headache of my life, every square inch of my brain throbbing with agony.

At first, I had no idea where I was. *Who* I was, even. I was just a mass of throbbing pain—unusually *bad* throbbing pain. Definitely not a hangover.

Aching, I opened my eyes, my vision blurry at first. All I could see was an enormous space with a raftered ceiling and the figure of a man.

A man?

*The killer.*

It was the killer. He stood just fifteen feet away, watching me. Waiting for me to wake.

And he'd seen me. The way his black eyes lit up made that perfectly clear.

Frantic, I tried to get out of the chair in which I seemed to be sitting. I was almost too weak to move, but it didn't matter. My wrists were bound to the back. I could stand, but I'd be bringing the chair with me.

I drew in a bracing breath and sat back, my mind spinning.

He hadn't killed me yet. Why?

I had no idea, but I needed to use it. How, though?

Distract him until help showed up. Yep. That made perfect sense. It was some pretty basic 101 you've-been-kidnapped-shit, but it was all I could think of.

"Why are you doing this?" I asked. "Why kidnap me?"

He laughed but didn't answer. Apparently, he wasn't going to lay out every detail of his dastardly plan. Well, a girl could always hope.

Instead, he walked forward. We had to be in the attic, as it was dusty and dark up here. The rafters overhead supported the sharply peaked roof, and there were a few windows on the side wall that led out to the ramparts.

The killer stepped into a beam of light, and I gasped. His hood was down, and now that I could see his face, he looked just like...

Like Lachlan.

"Who are you?" The words trembled as they escaped my lips.

"Surely you can guess."

His voice was cold, his eyes colder. They were completely black, with no whites at all. Cold iced me.

*His brother.* Garreth. "You're supposed to be dead."

He looked so different than I remembered. He'd been slight when I'd seen him last, not even an adult yet. Now, he was a hardened man. Almost as handsome as his brother, and almost as big, but a killer.

He nodded. "I *am* supposed to be dead. You're right. Brother dearest would agree with you, too. He saw my body."

"What happened?"

"Hmm, I don't think I'm going to tell you that."

"Then why did you take me?"

"I needed bait. I saw you with my brother, saw the way he looked at you, and knew he'd come for you."

It had never been about me at all.

He strolled closer, and I noticed that he was holding something in his hand. A leather cuff studded with potions.

"My cuff." My gaze caught on a silver charm dangling from a slender chain, and I gasped. "My necklace!"

He held them up and smiled. "Quite the interesting collection of jewelry you have."

I began to pant, panic making my limbs go numb.

Holy shit, holy shit, holy shit. He had my *necklace*.

"This leather one is quite obvious, though ingenious." He held it up to display it. Then he held up the chain. My pendant glinted in the narrow ray of sunlight. "This, however, was most unexpected."

"It's a comms charm." The lie was desperate and dumb, and he could tell.

"That's what I thought as well. Didn't want you calling for help, now did I?" He swung the charm, and my gaze followed it. "But as soon as I took it off, those ears of yours disappeared. They're round now. And your scent changed. Your entire signature." He strolled around me, and I shuddered. "You're a shifter. And if I'm not mistaken, you're not just any shifter."

"I'm not." My lies were sounding thin even to my own ears.

He came around to crouch in front of me. "You're my brother's mate. I'd recognize your signature anywhere. It surprised the hell out of me when you walked into our chambers all those years ago, so dowdy and plain but smelling like the best thing I'd ever run into."

I spat at him. I couldn't help it. Rage filled me up, and I spat at him.

He lunged backward, then slapped me so hard I saw stars. My head rang, and my eyes watered.

A crashing noise sounded from the far side of the attic, and he straightened abruptly, then spun to stride toward it.

Was help here?

He disappeared into the shadows at the far side, and I began to struggle anew, trying to tear my hands out of the rough rope bonds.

*Chill out!*

Ralph's little voice sounded in my head, and I glanced down, shocked to see him there. He looked dusty and worn out, but he started working on the ropes that held my hands.

I said nothing, not wanting Garreth to hear me talking to my familiar. Only I could hear Ralph's voice in my head.

*I've almost got you free, then you can run for it out the window. Or wait, and I'll try to find Lachlan.*

Desperately, I tried to telepathically send my thanks to Ralph. He'd clearly climbed up here somehow, then set off a distraction for Garreth. When I saw the man's huge shadow returning, I cleared my throat to warn Ralph. I felt the bonds fall away and heard the faint noise of his little footsteps as he ran off into the shadows. I hoped he'd taken the ropes with him so that they weren't sitting right under my chair.

Of course he had. Ralph was clever enough to find my entire stash—he'd take care of the details. And thanks to my little thief, my hands were free. Garreth was almost upon me, but I had options now.

"Why did you take me?" I asked. "Why not just kill me?"

He laughed, then spun in a circle, looking toward the door. My gaze followed his movements, and I noticed a string that formed a tripline in front of the threshold. Another string connected it to a spot deeper in the room...and led straight to a crossbow with a silver-tipped bolt.

*Bait.*

I was bait.

~

*Lachlan*

Eve.

Fear like I'd never known shot me straight in the heart. She'd been taken fifteen minutes ago, through a secret door that I'd had no idea existed, and we still hadn't found her. No one had been able to make the door reappear, and we'd abandoned the effort.

How the hell did the killer know the tower better than I did?

The search had taken on a new urgency, and her friends were as frantic as I was. But every room we searched, every cubbyhole, was empty.

I was stepping onto the eighth floor when I felt it.

*My mate.*

The knowledge of her hit me in the chest like a

battering ram, driving the breath from my lungs. Somehow, she had appeared. She was in this very tower. I could feel her like I could feel my own limbs. And she was in danger.

Eve?

It had to be Eve. I had no idea why I could feel her now, but I could.

"She's upstairs," I said, my gaze going to Seraphia. "Highest part of the tower."

"How do you know?"

"I can feel her." I rubbed my chest, then turned and raced for the stairs. I had to get to her.

~

*Eve*

Garreth watched me as I swallowed hard, my gaze riveted to the bolt. Silver. Poisonous to werewolves. A shot to the heart would kill Lachlan, *quickly*. A regular bolt might not—werewolves were powerful healers—but that silver bolt was deadly if it hit him in the right spot. Even if it didn't, it would weaken him, maybe even make them evenly matched.

"I assumed they would come for you," he said. "I'm not as strong as my brother, you see. No one is, especially when he's in his wolf form. So I need the upper hand. Little did I know I found his *mate*. He'll be able to sense you now that the necklace is off. He's coming for you."

*Oh, fates.*

I couldn't wait for help to arrive.

As subtly as I could, I reached into the ether and withdrew my bag. It was too big for me to be completely graceful about it, and Garreth noticed that something was up. His brow furrowed and he stepped forward. "What are you doing?"

I plunged my hand into the bag and yanked out the first potion bomb I could find, then lunged to my feet to hurl it at him.

But he was too fast and dodged. It shattered on the ground behind him, spraying green liquid everywhere. An acid bomb, wasted.

I shoved my hand in for another and hurled it, hitting him in the shoulder that time. The acid ate into his skin, green and bright. He howled but didn't go down.

The Dark Moon curse had to be making him stronger.

Behind him, the door opened. Lachlan appeared.

Before he could trip the wire, I screamed. "Duck! It's a trap!"

It was too late. He'd already stepped forward, and his foot caught the wire. But he seemed to have heard me. He ducked low and caught the bolt high on his shoulder. Pain flashed on his face as he yanked it free.

I pulled another potion bomb out and hurled it at Garreth. He dodged, his movements unnaturally fast, and turned to charge toward Lachlan.

My mate.

His gaze met mine, just briefly. I could feel him now.

With the pendant gone, I could feel Lachlan like a second heart.

It was insane.

Everything happened in the blink of an eye. Lachlan caught sight of Garreth, and his eyes widened with shock as he went white.

Garreth drew a long, wickedly sharp knife.

"Garreth." Lachlan's voice was rough.

"Brother."

"You were dead."

Garreth just smiled, cold and dark, then charged. He reached Lachlan and raised the knife.

Lachlan deflected it, landing a blow to his brother's gut. Garreth doubled over, gasping, but managed to swipe at Lachlan's arm with his blade.

The metal cut through Lachlan's jacket. He flinched, then dove at Garreth and drove him to the floor. Garreth's head cracked on the wood, and his arms went briefly slack. Seizing the opportunity, Lachlan grabbed the blade out of his brother's hand and chucked it across the room.

But Garreth soon recovered his strength and threw Lachlan off him. They grappled, rolling and punching, landing hit after vicious hit.

I grabbed a stunner potion bomb but couldn't find an opening. They moved too quickly, and I was just as likely to hit Lachlan.

Garreth managed to hurl Lachlan off of him once more before lunging for the discarded blade. He swept it up in his hand and turned toward Lachlan, blade raised high.

Lachlan's eyes flashed, and he shifted, transforming into his wolf. He was massive and glorious as he snarled, then lunged.

Clearly realizing he was outmanned when Lachlan was in wolf form, Garreth hurled the knife. He was an excellent shot, and the dagger sliced along Lachlan's front leg. Lachlan stumbled, and Garreth raced for the window, knowing he didn't stand a chance. I hurled another potion bomb, hitting him right in the back, but he didn't even stop. Tearing off his jacket, he scrambled to freedom.

Lachlan followed, leaping out the window seconds behind him.

Seraphia appeared in the doorway, looking around the attic in befuddlement.

"Watch out for traps!" I shouted as I ran after the brothers.

It was night already, the moon full. Garreth must

have transformed, because now there were two wolves on the roof. Lachlan, the larger of the pair, chased Garreth, their forms illuminated by the moonlight. He was nearly on him. I sprinted after them, knowing it was crazy to run toward a fight like this but unable to wimp out now.

Lachlan leapt, soaring four meters through the air, a feat of incredible ability that took my breath away. He landed on Garreth, and the two tumbled across the gently slanted roof, rolling over and over as they snarled and bit at each other. Flashes of blood gleamed in the pale light, marring both wolves. It was riveting. So violent. So powerful.

Panting, I slowed to a halt about twenty meters away. The fight was taking too long.

Lachlan should have won already. His brother was stronger and faster as a result of the Dark Moon curse, but not as strong as Lachlan. Even with his bolt wound, Lachlan should have been able to take him out...

*He doesn't want to kill his brother.*

The thought flashed into my mind so brightly that I felt like an idiot for not realizing it sooner.

Wolves weren't exactly great at taking hostages. It was more *kill or be killed* when they fought.

Frantic, I scrambled in my bag for a stunner potion. It had to be a stunner. Two of them. Nothing else would do, as I couldn't guarantee that I was going to hit the right wolf. They were a mass of flailing fur and limbs.

I found the first one, thank fates, then another. Quietly, I approached. The wolves were too distracted to dodge me, but I couldn't afford to miss. I stopped ten meters away, shaking. The fight was so vicious and powerful that it made my soul seem to shrivel up inside me.

Carefully, I aimed for the smaller wolf, then hurled my potion bomb. It landed square on his back. He gave one last bite toward Lachlan's shoulder, then collapsed, unconscious.

Panting, I dropped my hands to my knees and braced myself, staring at them. *Finally*, I'd landed one on that bastard.

It took Lachlan a moment to realize his brother was down. When he did, he lunged backward and transformed to human, shock on his face as he stared at the unconscious wolf.

"He's not dead!" I shouted.

Seraphia came up from behind me, holding out her hands so that the vines could grow from her palms. They stretched across the roof and wound around the wolf, wrapping him up in a bundle that he wouldn't be able to escape. When she was done, she handed me the silver chain and pendant that I'd lost. "Found it on the floor. He must have dropped it."

I stared down at it. To put it back on, or not?

Even now, I could feel the pull between Lachlan and me. The mate bond was impossible to ignore.

I took the coward's way out and put the necklace on. The bond broke immediately, and his gaze flashed to mine.

"Your ears are back," Seraphia murmured.

"Thanks." I stared at Lachlan, unable to look away. It was impossible to read his face, but my secret was definitely out. I swallowed hard, then stepped back.

He'd caught the killer. His *brother*.

"He should be unconscious for an hour," I said. "I have a truth potion. If you make him take it while he's weakened, he'll give more answers."

Lachlan nodded, his jaw tight.

Part of me wanted to run, but a bigger part of me wanted answers. *Needed* answers. What the hell had happened here?

Lachlan hoisted his brother in his arms and staggered toward me. As he neared, I caught sight of the blood soaking through his clothes. *So many wounds.* Garreth had landed quite a few grisly bites, and it hurt just to look at him.

"I can make the vines carry him down," Seraphia said.

"No." Lachlan's tone was so hard that she just nodded.

He passed us, carrying the wolf that was his brother. His expression was shattered, grief in every line of his face.

Seraphia reached for my hand and squeezed. I

looked over at her, feeling tears prick my eyes. "This is so much worse than I expected."

She nodded. "I know, love. But it's going to be okay."

"Not for Lachlan."

She sighed, her expression sad. "Maybe not."

I swallowed hard. "Let's go get this over with."

## 19

*Eve*

Lachlan brought Garreth down to the basement. To the same cell I'd been tossed into, in fact. Apparently, it was reserved for murderers.

At the door, he turned to Seraphia and me. "Give me a moment."

We nodded, and he shut the door.

While we waited, we sent a text to Carrow, letting her know that the search was done and everyone was fine. Well, mostly. She didn't need all the details.

A few minutes later, Lachlan opened the door. Behind him, I spotted Garreth, human once more, semi-conscious and bound with huge iron chains.

I looked at Lachlan. He met my gaze with eyes of steel. "The truth potion?"

I nodded and pulled it out of my leather cuff, which I'd found on the floor of the attic. "You should be able to get three or four questions out of him. Depends on how shit he's feeling right now. A healthy person, you'd get just one."

He nodded, his expression grim.

My heartbeat thundered as I followed him into the room. Seraphia made to follow, but Lachlan turned around and shook his head.

She nodded. "I'll be upstairs."

*He's letting me stay.*

I kept my distance as he pinched Garreth's nose and made him drink the potion, my heart breaking with every second I had to watch him. Memories of them as children flashed in my mind. I'd seen them occasionally from a distance, always together. Playing when they were younger, competing when they were older, but always together.

Why had Lachlan had to lose so much? I hated how unfair it was.

After he'd swallowed, Garreth blinked and sat upright, his black eyes still crazed.

Lachlan looked at me, and I nodded. "Go ahead. It works right away."

"Why did you kill them, Garreth?" he asked.

He clenched his jaw, resisting at first. Finally, he spat, "Erasing my past."

Lachlan didn't look surprised, just nodded. Bill and Danny must have been Garreth's friends as children, and Lachlan knew it. That also explained desecrating their father's grave and going after Lachlan.

My heart hurt just to think of it.

"Did you fake your own death?" Lachlan asked.

"No." He shook his head, stubbornness creasing the side of his mouth.

Confusion flashed on Lachlan's face, and he turned to me.

"The potion is still working," I said. Garreth's attention would be riveted to us until the effect wore off.

Lachlan turned back to his brother. "I saw your body. I *buried* your body. You would have had to plan that. We don't reanimate."

I frowned. What the hell was happening? Lachlan had buried his brother's body, yet he was here?

"What happened?" Lachlan demanded. "Tell me, damn it! What happened to you?"

"I don't know!" Garreth shouted, his black eyes wild. He struggled against his chains, and pain flickered over Lachlan's face.

It was true. Everything he was saying was true. He really didn't know how he'd survived the accident Lachlan had seen.

"Careful," I murmured. "Just one more question. Maybe two, but probably not."

He gave a short, bitter laugh. "Don't waste them, then?"

He looked like he was at the end of his line, his face tight with pain. He turned back to his brother. "Is it over, or are more people threatening our pack?"

It was the right question. The most selfless question. Lachlan was Alpha for a reason.

"There are more." Garreth nodded. "Many more. And they're coming. For her."

His gaze moved to me, so bright and intense that I shivered.

"Me?" I whispered, my skin chilled.

He laughed, crazed with the Dark Moon curse. "I felt it when I took the necklace off. She's the one we seek. The one *he* seeks."

"Who?" Lachlan demanded. "Who, goddamn it?"

Garreth shut his mouth, then leaned back against the wall and stared into space.

Shit. Shit. Shit.

The potion was done.

I looked at Lachlan. He turned to me, frustration creasing his mouth. "Do you have more of those potions?"

I shook my head. "Not here. And it will take time to make them."

"Fine." He gave his brother one last look, then

turned and left, gesturing for me to precede him out of the room.

Every inch of my body vibrated as I walked before him. I gave Garreth one last glance over my shoulder. He looked like hell.

"He'll need medical attention," I said.

"He'll get it." There was no anger in Lachlan's voice, just exhaustion. Sadness.

He shut the door behind him, closing Garreth in, and I turned to him, having no idea what I'd say.

"Not here." His tone was curt.

Well, that made it easy. I spun back around and marched up the stairs. On the main level, Kenneth and a woman waited for us. I'd seen her when the troops were organizing themselves for the search: Moira MacKenna, the leader of his security forces.

She met Lachlan's gaze. "He's in the dungeon?"

Lachlan nodded. "Kenneth, arrange medical treatment for him. And food. But use extreme caution. He's dangerous. The Dark Moon curse."

Moira frowned. "The curse? And we're not killing him?"

She didn't know it was Garreth.

Oh, fates.

"Not yet," Lachlan said.

"That's not protocol. You know it better than anyone."

She wanted him to kill his brother. *Now*.

No, no, no. I couldn't bear it.

"We will," Lachlan said, his voice totally devoid of emotion. "But not yet. He has information we need. If anyone does *anything* to him, they'll be banished."

Moira paled. Lachlan was at the end of his rope, and she could tell.

He met her gaze. "Assign the appropriate forces to help Kenneth, then see to it that the Shadow Guild members leave the premises immediately."

My heart lurched.

*I'm leaving.*

It was a good thing, of course. But I hated how torn up Lachlan looked. How broken.

Moira nodded and gestured for me to follow her.

"Not her." His voice was sharp.

She nodded and spun on her heel, departing. Kenneth was already gone.

"What do you mean, *not me*?" I asked. "I'm Shadow Guild."

"Are you, *mate*?"

I bristled. "I am now. And I had my reasons for my secrets."

"I don't care." His voice was harder than I'd ever heard it, sharper and colder. He gripped my arm, and I yanked, trying to pull away. "Stop," he said. "You'll bruise yourself."

"*You're* bruising me."

"You're right. I should be more careful." His eyes

were flinty as he swept me into his arms and threw me over his shoulder.

I landed with an *oomph*, the air rushing out of my lungs. Quickly, he gripped my cuffed wrist, holding it firmly so that I couldn't sneak a potion out to use in defense.

"Let me go, you bastard!" I kicked and thrashed, trying to break free.

"You're my mate, Eve." He strode through the halls and climbed the stairs that led to the top of the tower.

"That doesn't mean you can kidnap me. You don't own me!"

"And yet here you are." He reached the room where he'd kept me prisoner and set me down, then shoved me gently inside. He blocked the door, his body too broad to slip past. "You're part of this, no matter how much you want to deny it. And until we find out what's going on—why this person is after you—I'm not letting you out of my sight. You're staying here."

Shock rooted me to the spot as I stared at him. His eyes never left mine as he shut the door in my face and turned the lock.

I hope you enjoyed *Darkest Moon*! Want to find out what Eve is doing in the tower? Click here for a deleted scene that was meant to be the start of book 2 but didn't quite fit. Book 2, *Wild Hunt,* will be here in early March 2021. Click here to get the pre-order.

If you liked Damian from Magic Side, Chicago, then good news! He has his own series—Dragon's Gift: The Storm. Click here to get his book, Wicked Wish. It's a funny urban fantasy with a rebel heroine, a dark angel hero, a slow burn romance, and edge of your seat adventure.

**THANK YOU FOR READING!**

I hope you enjoyed reading this book as much as I enjoyed writing it. Reviews are *so* helpful to authors. I really appreciate all reviews, both positive and negative. If you want to leave one, you can do so at Amazon or GoodReads.

# ACKNOWLEDGMENTS

Thank you, Ben, for everything. There would be no books without you.

Thank you to Jena O'Connor and Ash Fitzsimmons for your excellent editing. The book is immensely better because of you! Thank you to Jenna Ossip-Klein and Susie J for your eagle eye with typos.

Thank you to my amazing narrator Laurel Schroeder for bringing the character's voices to life.

Thank you to Orina Kafe for the beautiful cover art and Chris Sim for the guild crests.

Hey there! I hope you enjoyed *Darkest Moon*. If you've read my Rebel series that starts with *Once Bitten*, you're probably familiar with Guild City. This series was inspired by research trips to Romania and London.

Before I get into the history, I should mention that Damian from Magic Side will be getting his own series at the end of February 2020! You may remember him from his appearance in Carrow's series (along with Nevaeh Cross). This series was written with my best friends, Veronica and Doug, who I met while I was an archaeologist. They write as Veronica Douglas. The book, *Wicked Wish*, is super fun and has a ton of cool history and archaeology (since that's their specialty, after all). Click here to check out their website to learn more about the book.

Guild City is based upon birthplace of Vlad the

Impaler, Sighișoara in Transylvania. It is a beautiful medieval city surrounded by a roughly circular wall that is listed as a UNESCO World Heritage Site. As with Guild City, there are towers built into the wall that were once owned and maintained by various guilds (such as the tailors, bookmakers, butchers, tinsmiths, and rope makers). The guild towers were responsible for the defense of the city when it came under attack, and each one is different and fascinating. As soon as I as I saw them, I was imaging Guild City.

On the English side of things, Richmond Park is a real park in London. It is the largest Royal Park at 2,500 acres and was established in the 1625 century by King Charles I as a place for deer. He enclosed it in 1637 and some of the walls still remain.

That's it for the history in this book, though I will go into more detail about the very cool guild towers in future books. Thank you for reading, and I hope you stick around with Eve and Lachlan to find out more.

## ABOUT LINSEY

Before becoming a writer, Linsey Hall was a nautical archaeologist who studied shipwrecks from Hawaii and the Yukon to the UK and the Mediterranean. She credits fantasy and historical romances with her love of history and her career as an archaeologist. After a decade of tromping around the globe in search of old bits of stuff that people left lying about, she settled down and started penning her own romance novels. Her Dragon's Gift series draws upon her love of history and the paranormal elements that she can't help but include.